Saving

Planet

Mary Arrigan

ATTIC PRESS
Dublin

First published in Ireland in 1995 by
Attic Press
29 Upper Mount Street
Dublin 2

ISBN 1 85594 178 3

A Catalogue record for this book is available from the British Library.

Cover illustration: Angela Clarke
Origination: Attic Press
Printing: Guernsey Press Co. Ltd

Attic Press receives financial assistance from the Arts Council/An Chomhairle Ealaíon.

Saving The Dark

Planet

About The Author

Mary Arrigan lives in Roscrea, Co Tipperary. She is the author of three further children's books, *Searching for the Green* (Attic Press), *Andy, Zeph and the Flying Cottage* (Hamish Hamilton), *Lá le Mamo* and *Mamo Cois Trá* (An Gum), and the 1993 winner of the Hennessy Award for best emerging writer.

Dedication

To Liz.

One

Many times, later on, Ashling recalled the events of that night. If only that stupid door had not been banging. If only her parents hadn't gone to comfort Nell, their close friend and neighbour. But it was the shed door she remembered most, as it went bang, bang, bang with annoying persistence. It had made her so cross that she turned on her ten year old sister as she fiddled with the knobs on the telly.

'Cara! Turn that telly off. Can't you see that the gale is causing interference? You're not going to get anything.'

'I'm trying to get MTV,' replied Cara, thumping the set.

'You're not going to get it,' snapped Ashling. 'Nor any other channel for that matter. Will you turn it off. I'm supposed to be studying for my Junior Cert. How can I do any work if you're mucking about? Can't you get it into your feeble brain that the telly is knackered? Now, switch it off.'

Cara made a face at her, but turned off the television. She went over to the window and peered out. The wind was howling across the night sky. Now and then the lights flickered as the electricity wires battled with the strong gusts.

'I hate this rotten storm,' she said. 'I bet the satellite dish has blown down. And listen to that door. Can you hear the door, Ash?'

The banging was louder now that the spluttering television had been turned off.

'Of course I can hear it,' said Ashling. 'I'm not deaf.'

'I bet it's the far barn door,' went on Cara. 'The hinges on that are rusty. It'll probably blow away.' She looked expectantly across at her sister.

'Well, what do you want me to do about it?' Ashling asked. She wished the silly door would blow away and give her some peace.

'Dad'll be furious,' said Cara. 'If the hay gets blown about and wet, he'll do a dance.'

'Go down yourself and fix it, if you're so worried.'

'We'll both go.'

'You're the one who's worried about it,' said Ashling. 'You go.'

'We were warned not to leave the house ...' began Cara.

'Well then, there's your answer,' replied Ashling triumphantly. 'Let the crummy door blow away to kingdom come for all I care. Now do you mind? I have work to catch up on and I'll never get it done if the light goes. I'm damned if I'm going to learn French verbs by candlelight.'

'You're a selfish cow,' protested Cara. 'It'll be more work for Dad if that door ...'

'Will you shut up about that door,' exclaimed Ashling. 'I'm sick of it and I'm sick of you.' She flung her French book on to the table. She musn't let Cara see that she was nervous.

'I wish Mam and Dad were here,' sighed Cara. 'Why couldn't they have waited until morning? A few hours won't make any difference whether Mr Brophy is found or not. He'll probably turn up. People don't just vanish.'

'But they do!' said Ashling, at last voicing her fear. 'Can't you get it into your head that three people have disappeared from this area alone, and four from the next county. No wonder everyone is scared witless.'

'All the more reason for Mam and Dad to stay with us,' pouted Cara.

'Well, think of poor Nell Brophy,' went on Ashling. 'She's on her own in the most isolated area and she doesn't know where her brother is.

I think our folks are just being normal good neighbours going to her like that. Now, will you find something to do, like get the candles from the dresser, just in case. And you could make supper for the two of us. Get a pizza from the freezer and shove it in the Aga. Good girl.'

'I'm going to shut that door,' Cara looked back at her sister defiantly as she stood on a chair at the dresser. 'You won't come because you're scared. Ashling is a scaredy cat.' She threw the candles on to the table.

'I am not.'

'Yes you are. You're afraid to come down the yard. Admit it.'

'Look, I'm not scared. I'll go down and fasten that crummy door. Will that satisfy you?'

'I'll come with you ...'

'No. You'll stay here. We were told not to leave the house. There's no need for the two of us to break our word. Put on the pizza. I'll be back in a tick. If I've to listen to that banging for much longer, I'll go berserk.'

'Berserk,' said Cara.

'What?'

'Berserk. The word is berserk.'

'That's what I said. Why don't you listen? Anyway, I'm going down to shut that door.'

'Come off it, Ash,' Cara looked anxious. 'Let me come too.'

Ashling shook her head. She took her anorak from the back of the kitchen door. She didn't really want to venture down the yard, but she wasn't about to lose face to a kid like Cara. It was satisfying to see her worried face. 'Lock the door after me.'

'I want to come too,' persisted Cara.

'Are you afraid to stay here alone?' Ashling said with relish.

'Go on, then. Hurry up.'

Ashling walked with forced confidence across the yard; she knew Cara would be watching from the window. Before reaching the cluster of sheds beyond the yard, she ducked out of the light and doubled back to the house. She grinned when she saw Cara through the open curtains. She was rooting in the freezer for the pizza. She'd teach the kid a lesson. With her death's head ring she scratched at the glass. 'Oooooooohhhhhh,' she wailed. 'Caaarrrraaaaa.' She pressed her face against the window and blew out her cheeks. Cara looked up, her face white and startled.

'It's meeee, the grey banshee,' shrieked Ashling. 'I'm coming for you, Caaarrraaaa.'

Cara's face relaxed. 'You stupid moron,' she shouted. 'Anyway, I knew it was you.'

'You did not,' Ashling yelled back over the wind. 'You were scared out of your tiny mind. I saw you. You were almost fainting, you wimp.'

But Cara had drawn the curtains. Ashling chuckled to herself as she made her way across the yard again. She wasn't at all frightened now. Scaring others was a good way of fighting off one's own fears, she must remember that in future.

The dark shapes of the sheds didn't seem so ominous now. Not really. However, she shivered slightly when she was out of range of the comforting yard light. Not that it was exactly pitch dark; there was a moon trying to shine behind the scudding clouds and, when her eyes became accustomed to the gloom, it was possible to make out familiar landmarks. Where was that stupid banging door? She hoped it wasn't one of the farthest sheds. Now she could make out the shapes of the buildings. The big shed that housed the cattle was well secured. She could hear them stomping restlessly. They didn't normally do that. Must be the wind has them disturbed, she told herself.

Mooo. Ashling leapt as the cattle set up a chorus of anxious bellowing. MOOOOOOOOO.

'Shut up, blast you,' she shouted, to relieve the fright. Her voice sounded tiny in the strong wind. 'I must be daft to be scared of a crowd of silly cows.' The banging door was attached to one of the smaller sheds beside the haybarn. Ashling skipped across the yard, glad that she didn't have to search further. Just as she reached the door, the light went out. The darkness was like a bucket of ink thrown over the whole farm. Though she had been out of range of the light, its comforting glow had been behind her. Now there was only herself and the black and grey shadows out in the windy night.

'Cara, I'll strangle you!' she shouted angrily. 'Always have to get your own back, don't you!' She fastened the door and checked that the bolt was secure. At least she'd got the job done, she consoled herself. She wished her parents would come home. But then she thought of Nell Brophy. Her brother had been missing since early morning. Normally that wouldn't be something to fuss about, but everyone was so scared about the disappearance of three others from the locality that one had only to go for a walk and the whole village would be out looking for you.

There was probably a perfectly logical explanation, Ashling reasoned as she made her way back across the dark yard. The cattle were still restless and she glanced towards their shed. As she did so, a shadowy shape slipped across the doorway and around the corner. Ashling froze. Had she imagined it? Bad enough to be out here in the gloom without imagining things. There it was again - or was it another one? It came from behind an old, disused shed and merged with the shadowy buildings.

Ashling felt a strange sensation on the back of her neck. Then reason intervened before she panicked. Cara! It had to be Cara. Of course, she laughed to herself with relief. The sneak, she'd turned out the yard light and followed her.

'Cara, I know it's you. If you think I'm scared, you have another think coming!' She certainly wouldn't let on that she HAD been frightened. She ran to the recess between the two sheds. 'I know you're in there,' She shouted. 'You might as well come out. I'm going back to the house and I'll lock the door. See how you'll like being out here all night!'

The wind blew the clouds momentarily from in front of the moon. The sudden bluish glow changed the shapes in the yard and revealed two silvery figures watching Ashling from the far end of the recess.

'Dear God!' she gasped.

She didn't know how her legs got the strength to start running. She wanted to scream, but no sound would come. Through puddles and pot-holes, she sped in her panic. Cara, turn on the blasted lights, she thought. She panted as she sprinted the last few steps to the dark, silent house. She turned the handle of the back door. It was locked.

'Cara! Cara, let me in!' There was no reply. She ran to the window and rapped so hard she thought it would break. 'Cara!' she was screaming now. 'Open the damn door!' Oh lord, maybe they'd got Cara. 'Cara!' She almost sobbed with relief as a glow came towards the window. The curtains were pulled back and Cara's grinning face looked out at her in the light of the candle she was holding.

'Oh, thank God. Cara, open the door ...'

'Sorry,' shouted Cara. 'You'll have to join your banshee sisters ...'

'Open the door. There are strange people after me ...'

'Of course there are,' laughed Cara. 'Heavy-metal leprechauns. Enjoy yourself out there. And see if you can fix up the electricity while you're at it.'

Ashling hammered at the window, sobbing with frustration.

'If I have to break the window, I will. For goodness' sake, Cara I'm not joking. There are weirdoes ...' She stopped. Cara's expression had changed. She was looking beyond her sister. Fearfully Ashling looked over her shoulder. Two slender shapes were barely visible against the mottled sky as they emerged from the shadows of the sheds. Cara seemed to be frozen.

'Cara, open up! Quick!' Cara jumped and opened the window, pulling her sister through. Without pausing for breath, they both fastened the old-fashioned shutters across the window and slotted the metal bar that held them in place.

'All the shutters!' cried Ashling. 'We must fasten all the

shutters.'

They ran through the house together, pulling out the shutters, most of which hadn't been used in years.

'Who are they?' panted Cara as they groped their way downstairs.

'I didn't stop to ask,' snorted Ashling. 'They were watching me from behind the old shed. I thought it was you, then I saw there were two of them. They were just standing there, watching. It was awful. Weird. I don't know how I got back to the house.'

'We'll ring the gardai,' said practical Cara. 'Then we'll ring Mam and Dad.'

'You needn't tell the parents that I was outside,' said Ashling, thinking ahead. No point in inviting a scolding later on. She held the candle while Cara dialled. She looked anxiously up at her sister and dialled again. 'It's dead,' she said. 'There's no sound at all.'

'Oh, Cara, you're joking.' Ashling took the phone from her and groaned as she put it to her ear. The silence was frightening. Now they were cut off, with God knows what louts outside. She looked at Cara with dismay.

'Perhaps they'll go away,' said Cara hopefully.

Ashling shook her head. She read the papers and watched the news on telly; she knew that the sort of people who robbed old people in their isolated farmhouses were vicious thugs who would not be put off by locked doors. Two youngsters cut off with no phone would not pose a threat to those scumbags.

She looked at her young sister whose face was white and frightened in the candlelight.

'We'll fight them,' she said with a rush of protectiveness. 'If they succeed in getting in, we'll skewer their guts to the wall.' She climbed on to a chair and felt along the top of the dresser.

'What are you looking for?' asked Cara, holding the candle aloft.

'Daddy's gun.'

'No!' protested Cara. 'You'd be up for ... for murder.'

'Pah! Murder me eye,' snorted Ashling. 'Shooting's too good for the likes of those. They'd kill a ninety year-old for his miserable pension.' She glanced at Cara and was sorry she'd said that. Now the kid was really scared. She was, after all, only ten and didn't have Ashling's street cred. The two sisters were as different as sisters could possibly be; Ashling was outgoing, prone to getting into trouble and would prefer listening to heavy metal to doing boring old homework. For Ashling life would be a lark if only drab grown-ups wouldn't get in the way.

Cara was small for her age, she actually liked school and all that stuff and was deadly serious about most things. 'An easy child to have around,' Mam would say, casting veiled looks at her older daughter. 'Keeps her room clean, not like the bomb site some people call a bedroom.'

'That's because she spends most of her time in there with her equally weird side-kicks playing weird computer games,' Ashling would retort.

She was feeling along the top of the dresser.

'It's not here. Where is it?'

'Oh, I remember,' said Cara, almost with relief. 'It's in the car. He was shooting rabbits yesterday.'

'Blast!' said Ashling.

'Sshh,' Cara put her finger to her mouth. They both froze. Very slowly the handle of the back door was turning. Ashling reached out and grasped Cara's arm. She put her other hand over her own mouth to stop herself from crying out.

'Good job the door was locked,' whispered Cara.

Ashling looked frantically around the kitchen. There must be something for them to use to fend off those thugs. Her eyes lit on the hurleys propped against the washing machine. She was on the junior camogie team at school and sometimes she and Dad practised shots out in the yard. She grabbed a hurley and handed the other to Cara.

'Aim for their knees and shins,' she said. Cara nodded. She wished she was as brave as Ashling. And she wished Mam and Dad would come home and that the electricity and phone would be fixed quickly. She felt Ashling squeeze her arm as a noise at the window indicated that the intruders were looking for another way in. How long would the double glazing and the shutters hold them off? They might even give up and go away. She sighed.

'They must have gone around to the front,' whispered Ashling as the stealthy movements stopped and all they could hear was the wind. 'Let's sneak into the hall. Leave the candle here.'

They eased open the door leading to the hall. The cold air hit them with a blast after the Aga-warm kitchen.

'Ssshh,' said Ashling. They gripped one another as they saw shadowy movements at the glass panel of the front door. This was too much for Cara. She broke from Ashling and ran closer to the door.

'Go away!' she shouted. 'We've rung the gardai and they're on their way. We have a gun here and we'll shoot.'

Ashling bit her lip. After hearing a child's voice, those thugs would guess that there were no adults here. However, there was no point in giving out to Cara now; the deed was done. She clutched her hurley firmly and went to stand beside her sister.

The movement at the door ceased. Cara turned towards her in the gloom.

'That seems to have scared ...' she began.

There was a splintering sound and shards of glass flew into the hall. Ashling and Cara leapt back. A hand came through the broken pane. Ashling raised the hurley to slam it down on the outstretched fingers but, in the reflected glow from the open kitchen door, she saw that this was not like any hand she had ever seen before. This was no human hand.

and [illegible] [illegible] [illegible], quickly. She felt Andy's [illegible] arm as a mood of [illegible] window [illegible] that the [illegible] were looking [illegible] [illegible] [illegible]. [illegible] [illegible] the [illegible] and the shutters hold them out? They might [illegible] [illegible] go away. She sighed.

'[illegible] must have gone around to the front window. [illegible] as the [illegible] [illegible] [illegible] [illegible] [illegible] could [illegible] [illegible] the [illegible]. [illegible] [illegible] into the hall, [illegible] [illegible] the [illegible].

They moved apart, the door leading to the hall. The [illegible] [illegible] them [illegible] [illegible] [illegible] the [illegible] kitchen.

'[illegible] [illegible] nothing.' They [illegible] [illegible] [illegible] they saw [illegible] [illegible] [illegible] at the glass panel of the front door [illegible] [illegible] [illegible] [illegible] she [illegible] [illegible] nothing and [illegible] closer to the door.

[illegible] [illegible] [illegible]. 'We're [illegible] the [illegible] [illegible] [illegible] [illegible]. We have a [illegible] [illegible] [illegible] about.'

[illegible] [illegible] [illegible] [illegible] [illegible], [illegible] [illegible] [illegible] [illegible] [illegible] that [illegible] [illegible] [illegible] [illegible]. However, [illegible] [illegible] [illegible] [illegible] [illegible]. [illegible] [illegible] [illegible] [illegible] [illegible] [illegible] [illegible] [illegible] and [illegible] [illegible] [illegible].

The [illegible] at the [illegible] and [illegible] turned towards her in the gloom.

'[illegible] [illegible],' she [illegible].

There was a [illegible] sound and shards of glass flew into the hall [illegible] and [illegible] back. A [illegible] through the [illegible] [illegible] [illegible] raised the [illegible], [illegible] on the [illegible] [illegible] [illegible] the [illegible] [illegible] the [illegible] [illegible]. [illegible] saw that [illegible] was the [illegible] she had ever seen before. [illegible] [illegible] [illegible].

Two

Ashling pulled Cara back from the splintering glass.

'Upstairs,' she hissed urgently.

Cara looked for a moment at the glass fragments shattering around her feet. Inside her head she wanted to cry out and to smash whoever was out there invading her family's space, but fear seemed to have frozen her into immobility. She was jolted back to reality as Ashling pulled her roughly by her jumper.

'I said upstairs,' Ashling hissed again. Cara knew her big sister was right. With all their strong intentions of fighting off these intruders, they both knew that their efforts would be futile. All that mattered was self-preservation. They fled together up the dark stairs as the tinkling glass echoed frighteningly in the hallway.

'The hot press,' whispered Ashling, still pulling Cara after her. The hot press had always been a favourite spot for games of hide-and-seek. It was a large, walk-in cupboard with shelves up to the ceiling. On the upper shelves were stored extra duvets and blankets.

'Up on to the top shelf quickly,' ordered Ashling. 'Stand on my back and feel your way behind the blankets. Pull them around you and don't make a sound.'

'What about you ...?' began Cara.

'I'll climb on to the second shelf. Don't waste time. Come on, up.'

She bit her lip as Cara's shoes dug into her back. When she reached the top shelf Ashling pushed her the rest of the way.

'Are you in?' she asked as she groped in the dark.

'Yes,' came the muffled reply.

'Good. Don't make a sound. No matter what happens, don't make a sound.' With that Ashling eased herself on to the second shelf and burrowed in behind the lagging jacket on the cylinder. Feeling about, she pulled a duvet around her, leaving an opening just wide enough to let in air. Downstairs the sound of breaking glass was replaced by heavy thuds. They were breaking down the rest of the door. Ashling bit her fist as she recalled the hand which she had briefly glimpsed. Who or what was breaking into their house? It was like something in a horror movie except that it was really happening.

'Ash, I'm scared.' Cara's voice came through the laths of the shelf above. 'What do those rotten sods want?'

Ashling took a deep breath. At least Cara hadn't noticed that the hand was different; she still thought that it was thieves who were out there. Better to let her believe that or she might go to pieces.

'Just keep very quiet,' Ashling whispered. 'They'll probably take a few things and go away.'

'I hope they don't take my Nintendo!' exclaimed Cara. 'If I hear them going near my room I'll ...'

'You'll do nothing. Like I said, keep absolutely still and keep your mouth shut. They'll go away soon.'

The thumping, splintering sound stopped and the sudden silence was the eeriest thing Ashling had ever experienced. What was happening now?

Where were those ... those things? She snuggled deeper into the duvet and felt that her heartbeat must be audible all over the house. Above her head Cara sniffled loudly. Ashling grimaced. 'Ssshhh' she whispered in the direction the sound had come from.

'I can't help it,' came the soft reply. 'My nose is running.'

'Well, wipe it on the blanket then.'

'Yecchh. Mam'll have my life ...'

'Just shut up, Cara. Please. Not another word.'

There were things being moved about downstairs.

They're looking for us, thought Ashling desperately. They're pulling things out to look for us. Oh, God, get me out of this and I'll be very good. I'll be a missionary and work with lepers.

The sounds of furniture being moved about was replaced by a different sound now; a soft, slithery sound. Ashling's heart leapt as a stair creaked. That was the fifth step from the bottom; it always creaked. They were coming upstairs, those creatures. She felt the top of her head to make sure it was covered. She hoped Cara was well covered too, and that she'd stay quiet.

The slithering noise passed along the corridor and a door squeaked softly. That was Mam and Dad's room. She wished Mam and Dad were here. They would have known how to handle this situation. Or would they? Perhaps it was just as well they weren't here, they would confront these things and probably get killed. What if they come back in the middle of all this? Would she run downstairs and warn them if she heard the car?

Would she scream at them to get help? What would be the sensible thing to do? She wished she could think clearly.

The door squeaked again. Dear Lord, let them think we've run out the back door. Cara sniffed again. Ashling felt she wanted to thump her; let her stupid nose run, it didn't matter about that. What was important was to keep very quiet. Her heart began to thump again as the slithery sound came back along the corridor. Go on, she wanted to shout. Keep going. It stopped outside the hot press. She pressed her hands to her face as if to make herself invisible and felt her stomach lurch as the door eased open. There was a noise, a sort of wheezy breathing, like her friend Alma when she had an asthma attack. Something was feeling the duvet that covered her. She held her breath and shut her eyes tight, as if, in doing so, she'd have extra defence. The cover was pulled away and Ashling screamed with terror. She could see nothing, but she could feel a presence that was all the more frightening because it was something unknown.

'Go away!' her voice shook. 'Go away whoever you are.' She prayed that Cara would keep still. That was her last conscious thought. Something grabbed the back of her neck and she felt herself falling into a deep, dark pit.

Ashling came to with a dry feeling in her throat. Her head ached and she wondered if she ought to go downstairs for a drink. As she looked around her gloomy surroundings, she realised with a jolt that she was not in her own room. The terrifying memories of the past few hours rushed into her mind. It had been no nightmare; it was real.

Cara! Where was Cara? All the normal antagonism felt by a teenage girl towards a younger sister disappeared as she was overcome by a deep sense of responsibility for the child.

She looked desperately around for Cara and found her, still asleep, curled up behind her. There were other people in a state of drowsiness lying about. They were in a small, round room with no windows. The walls were metallic which lent a cold atmosphere to the dim interior. There were no seats, but grey cushions were scattered around the floor. A humming sound made Ashling want to hold her head. Where had those creatures gone? She sat up and looked at the people around her. They were human, thank goodness. One of them stirred and was sitting with his head in his hands. Even in the dim light she recognised those strong shoulders that had often given her piggy backs when she was very young.

'Mr Brophy!' she exclaimed. 'Is that you Jack Brophy?'

His familiar figure was comforting in this strange place. He was a stockily built man with big, capable hands that could mend anything, from Ashling's bike to her father's tractor. He had a square, determined jaw that gave him an air of confidence. A man you could depend on. His hair was receding slightly and he'd always reminded Ashling of Bob Hoskins in 'Mermaids'. She once told him that and he'd roared laughing.

When his sister's husband died suddenly, Jack Brophy had taken her back to live on the family farm in partnership with him. They were both very good friends of Ashling's parents. Their old farmhouse, full of interesting nooks and rooms with sloping ceilings, was as much home to Ashling and Cara as their own home.

'Jack!'

He turned and she saw the look of anxiety cross his face.

'Young Ashling,' he said, peering at her in the half light. 'I can't say I'm glad to see you, lass. How did you get caught up in this?'

Ashling told him. She told him how her parents were, at this very moment, comforting his sister.

'Perhaps if I hadn't gone out to shut that blasted door those scumbags would have just gone away. Now I've got Cara involved as well,' she added miserably.

'Don't blame yourself,' soothed Jack. 'These fellows know exactly what they want and nothing can stop them.'

'Who are they, Jack? What do they want with all these people?' she gestured at the reclining forms of the others.

'Wish I could answer that,' sighed Jack. 'All I can remember is that one moment I was ushering the cows out of the milking parlour and the next I woke up in this place. There are eight of us here now. We all seem to have been knocked out in some way. No one has come to tell us why we're here or where we're going. The only time the door slides open is when more drugged people are thrown in.'

By now others were beginning to come to and were looking about them in dismay. There were, as Jack Brophy said, about eight people, of whom Ashling and Cara were obviously the youngest. The others ranged in age from about seventeen to forty and there seemed to be only one woman.

The boy of seventeen stretched himself and got up. Ashling recognised him as Lou Gaffney, a fifth year student from her community school. He was always getting medals for hurling and rugby and stuff; the sort of boy Ashling pretended not to like simply because she knew he wouldn't look twice at her. Girls fought with one another for the honour of being part of Lou's popular clique.

His hair was longish, bleached on top and dark underneath which earned him the nickname 'Cool Guinness'. Ashling had often watched him strutting about the playing field, his tight tee-shirt straining against his muscles, and fantasized about him coming over to sit just with her. She'd become so popular and everyone would want to know her because she was Lou's special friend. Then she'd sigh and realise that the Lou Gaffneys of this world were way out of her league. Blushing near-fifteen year olds didn't fit into his scene.

He was making his way over. Ashling was glad it was gloomy so that he wouldn't notice the blush creeping over her face. She pressed her fingers into her palms. Here she was, with her kid sister, in some sort of metal can being abducted by weirdoes and all that was bothering her was that Lou Gaffney might notice her blushing! Ashling, you're a right eejit, she thought.

'Hi, Mr Brophy,' he said. 'What the hell is going on?'

Jack Brophy shrugged his shoulders. 'Haven't a clue, son. How did you get here?'

'Going home from training after school. I was just at the forest gate, half a mile from my own house, when something shot through the spokes of my bike and threw me. I'm just coming round now. At least, I think I'm coming round. Is this a dream, by any chance?'

'Wish it was,' said Jack. 'I haven't even seen whoever our abductors are.'

'Where are they taking us? What do they want us for?' Lou rubbed his eyes as if to see better in the dim light.

'Haven't a clue.' said Jack. He nodded towards the other people. 'We're hardly a negotiable commodity.'

'Maybe they're some sort of terrorists,' ventured Lou.

'They're not terrorists,' put in Ashling.

'What?' Both men turned. God, she wished she'd said nothing. Now they were both looking at her. She swallowed and tried to think cool so that the blush would disappear.

'They ... they're not like us. Not like people. They're some kind of creatures.'

'You saw them?' Lou was looking at her intently. She nodded and looked at Jack in case the words would come out wrong if she spoke to Lou.

'The one who grabbed me had slimy hands. I saw his hand when it broke the glass on our front door. It was all scaly ...'

Lou laughed harshly. 'Come off it, sweetheart. You've been watching too many sci-fi videos. They're terrorists holding us hostage, I'm telling you. Creatures me granny!' and he laughed again.

Ashling's face was burning, but this time from anger. 'I saw him. I even felt him,' she insisted. 'I was hiding in the hot press with Cara and this ... this creature pulled the duvet away. I felt his awful hand on the back of my neck. I'm telling you - these people are not human.'

Lou began to laugh again, but Jack Brophy shook his head at him.

'Are you sure, Ashling?' he asked kindly.

'Of course I'm sure. What humans have hands like that?'

'Could have had gloves on,' Lou ignored her and directed his remark to Jack. 'Rough gardening gloves or something.'

'Oh, be like that, then,' Ashling surprised herself with her own snappiness. She saw that Cara was stirring and was glad of the excuse to leave the two men. That Lou, he made her feel a right fool. She wondered if he was right; had she imagined that the hand was scaly? The sod, let him think what he liked. She WAS right. How could she forget the terror she'd felt staring at that hand?

'Ashling, is that you?' Cara was rubbing her head.

'Yep, it's me, your lovely sister,' she tried to sound cheerful. 'And your next question is, where are we? and my answer is, I don't actually know, but there are lots of people here with us.'

Cara looked around the metal chamber. 'What's that humming noise?' she asked.

'It sounds like some sort of a generator,' Ashling answered. 'Though, if it is, it's not giving out much electricity. Are you all right?' She cupped Cara's face in her hands in a protective gesture.

'I'm sure we'll be out of here in no time at all. Look, Jack Brophy is here too.'

As they turned, a door slid open and a thin figure was silhouetted in the light. An orange glow emanated from his eyes. Everyone froze.

'Good grief!' exclaimed Lou.

'What the hell ..?' intoned Jack.

Ashling was far too frightened to feel triumphant. She rather wished that Lou had been right, that it was terrorists. However vicious, at least they'd be human. This creature and this place filled her with a deep, cold terror of something beyond all understanding.

Three

The figure at the door was joined by three others. One of them pressed a switch on the wall and the light became brighter. There was a gasp from the surfacing sleepers as the figures came clearly into vision. They were shaped like humans and wore what looked like streamlined tracksuits of some light material. Their faces were pale and scaly in texture. Their noses were squashed almost level with their cheekbones and their mouths were thin and colourless. They had three fingers and a thumb on each hand. Their eyes were large and would have appeared reptilian were it not for the warm, orange glow emanating from them. Their hair grew in short, matted tufts. Ashling noted that one of the figures was that of a woman, at least it looks like a woman, she thought. She felt she should have been comforted by that, but she wasn't. One of the figures stepped forward and spoke.

'We hope you're recovering,' he said in perfect English. 'You have been in a state of hypnotic sleep for twelve hours, your time. We are taking you to a place beyond your galaxy. You must stay calm. Not to do so could lead to imploding blood vessels. There is sufficient oxygen for all and nourishment will be supplied. Do not attempt to leave this chamber.'

Everyone began clamouring at once, to find out where they were, where they were being taken and why. The creature held up his three-fingered hand for silence. His companions moved closer to him as if to protect him.

'We are not evil people. We are very much like you. All

will be revealed to you in good time.' His eyes wandered around the disbelieving group and lit on Jack Brophy.

'You,' said the figure. Jack pointed to himself with surprise.

'Me?'

'Yes. You are the oldest. Come with us.'

'Don't go, Jack,' said Ashling. 'I don't trust those ...'

'She's right,' Lou put out his hand. 'Tell him to buzz off.'

But Jack Brophy shook his head. 'It's all right,' he said. 'I don't think I'll come to any harm. Unless, of course they've got a pot of water on to make Brophy soup.' He forced a smile and made his way across the room. At the door he turned and waved.

'Oh, God. I wish he hadn't gone,' said Ashling. 'This is what will happen. They'll take us out one by one for ... for ...'

Lou came and sat close to her. 'Jack Brophy will sort them out, you'll see. If they try anything physical, he'll lay them flat. They look like wimps. I hate wimps.' He fiddled with his shoelaces for a moment and looked sheepishly at Ashling. 'You were right after all. I really thought you were cracking up when you mentioned creatures with slimy hands. This is, like, science non-fiction.' He looked at her with a reassuring grin. There was a mark where one of his front teeth had been chipped and filled. Probably a rugby injury, thought Ashling. If the rest of 3A could see her now, sitting in some sort of space thing with Lou Gaffney chatting to her. This was all unreal.

Over all the confusion in her head there was a fearful premonition that things would never be the same again. She longed for the familiar security of home. Part of her felt like a helpless child, another part of her realised that this was no time for childish panic; she must be grown up, must look after her sister.

'Where are we going, do you think?' piped Cara. 'I think I'm going to throw up.'

'You only think that,' said Ashling. 'Take a deep breath and you'll be OK.'

Everyone was now awake, their faces still full of disbelief. Cara took to wandering among them, her discomfort obvious from her gait.

She glanced anxiously back at Ashling, her face white and pinched.

'I did what you said,' her voice was shrill. 'But I still want to throw up.'

'Here, lass,' a man was pointing to a door with a figurative symbol on it. 'I think this might be what you're looking for.'

There was a panel beside the door and, when the man touched it, the door slid open. It was indeed a toilet. Cara looked in doubtfully. She was afraid to go in.

'Come on, then,' sighed Ashling. 'It's only a fancy lav.'

Cara put her hand to her mouth and shook her head.

'Brave kid like you afraid to go to the bathroom?' laughed Lou.

Ashling glanced at him, surprised at his lack of sympathy for the little girl.

'Here, I'll stand outside,' said a bearded young man, rising to awkwardly guide the scared child to the sliding door. Ashling smiled gratefully at him as she reached her sister. He had a nice enough face, but it was spoiled by a disagreeable expression, as if he wanted to distance himself from everyone in the room. His hair was tied back in a ponytail and he sported one earring which he was twisting nervously. He nodded to Cara and posted himself outside the door.

'Ta,' said Ashling, but he didn't look at her or respond. Ashling shrugged and followed her sister into the small, metallic washroom. Apart from a tiny sink and a WC, there was nothing else, not even a towel. She splashed Cara's face with the tepid water and tried to console her as she cleaned her up .

'They can't keep us here for long,' she said as she stroked Cara's damp hair off her clammy forehead.

'But who are they?' asked Cara. 'I'm really scared, Ash. I wish ...'

'Hush,' soothed Ashling. She swallowed back her own deep fear. 'I'll ... I'll look after you. And there's Jack,' she added with a note of relief. 'Jack will see us through this. Don't worry, Car. We'll be OK.'

She knew her words were inane, but she could think of nothing else to say.

When they returned to the main chamber, everyone immediately fussed over Cara. At least the kid's discomfort has broken the ice, thought Ashling. Stories were now being shared of how people were abducted: walking in the country; driving a trailer of rubbish to the council tip; waiting for the bus to town, ordinary, everyday things. All had one thing in common; all had been taken in isolated areas.

'How did you get here?' someone asked the bearded young man, trying to get him to join in the talk. He fidgeted with his earring again before replying. He had a gruff, grudging voice as if he didn't want to speak. 'I was on my way to fish in the lake this morning. One minute I was casting a fly and the next I wake up here. Took me by surprise.'

Lou looked at him with an air of superiority.

'Well of course. It took us all by surprise,' he scoffed. 'How else would they have spirited us up here? If I'd seen them I certainly wouldn't be here now. I'd have fought them off.'

The young man scowled and shrank back into his denim jacket. Ashling wondered why Lou had put him down so rudely.

'What do you suppose they want from us?' someone asked.

Nobody could answer that, and an uneasy silence fell on the group.

The only other female stood up. She was in her thirties, Ashling supposed. She had her auburn hair cut very short. Except for her beautiful eyes which were open and frank and outlined by long lashes, she had what Mam would call a handsome face rather than a pretty one. She was wearing a navy jumper and a green skirt. Her quiet air of authority inspired confidence.

'My name is Elizabeth,' she said. 'I'm a doctor. I think we must get to know one another. We're probably going to be together for a long time.'

'We hope,' muttered the bearded man, nodding towards the door through which Jack had been taken. 'We hope they'll leave us together, I mean.' He was sitting on his own again, apart from the main group, with his arms around his knees. His face was tense and, when he spoke he looked at no one, keeping his eyes on the ground. His beard did little to hide the grim line of his mouth. His dark eyes, when he did raise them above ground level, were guarded and almost hostile.

His remark caused more worried frowns. What was happening to Jack Brophy? Would others be selected and called out? How could one fight this awful fear? An uneasiness crept into the atmosphere.

'You're making it sound like a party, lady,' Lou broke the silence with a forced laugh. 'Let's all get to know one another, like at some crummy party. That's not going to be much use if these slimeballs are going use us for some sort of scientific experiments.'

'What?' Cara's face paled and she clung to Ashling. 'What's he saying, Ash? Are they going to cut us open to look inside us?'

Ashling looked at Lou with disbelief. Surely he couldn't mean that?

'You stupid bloody moron,' another man rebuked him. 'We're stuck here whether we like it or not. There is nothing we can do about it. Elizabeth is right; our only defence is ourselves. If you start a bloody panic, we'll fall apart. Cop yourself on.'

Others nodded their heads in agreement. But Lou was unmoved. His glance swept over the group.

'Look at us all,' he said. 'We're just sitting there like lame ducks waiting for these ... these things to claim us. I certainly don't intend to go down without a fight. It's everyone for himself.'

'Would you have us run about thumping the walls and screaming our heads off?' asked Elizabeth. 'That would really help, wouldn't it?'

'Better than just sitting here,' began Lou.

'Cool it,' the bearded young man snarled in a low voice to Lou. 'No point in scaring folks.'

Lou looked at him disdainfully. 'Make me,' he said. A look of hatred passed between them.

'Stop fighting,' put in another man with a quiet voice. He was strongly built and his face had the weathered look of someone who spends a lot of time outdoors. 'This will get us nowhere. If we can just stay calm and see what's happening. We're all puzzled and frightened, but we must help one another. My name is Dan Leary. I'm an organic farmer ...'

'What's that?' Cara asked.

Dan Leary smiled and ruffled Cara's hair. His jeans were grubby, as if he had been in the middle of working on the land when he'd been taken. He gestured with his squarish hands as he spoke.

'It means that I grow all sorts of vegetables without the use of sprays and chemical stuff like that,' he explained patiently to the serious-faced little girl. 'Old-fashioned methods of farming.'

'Why?' asked Cara. Ashling nudged her. Did she always have to be so curious, even at a time like this?

'Because all those sprays and things can have harmful effects on people,' put in Elizabeth. 'Isn't that so, Dan?'

Dan nodded. 'That's it in a nutshell,' he said. 'Poisonous gunge.'

Dan's forthright attitude spread to the others. Introducing themselves kept them from sinking into their private fears, and the sound of human voices was comforting in this incredible situation.

'My name is Ian and I'm an engineer.' Ashling turned to where a tall, gangling man was speaking. He wore Timberland boots and Levis. His shirtsleeves were rolled up to reveal tanned arms. He wore a corduroy waistcoat that emphasised his leanness. Two days' stubble on his face gave him the air of one also used to the rough outdoors. Ashling thought him rather nice, especially when he added, with a fleeting grin, 'And I play bass guitar with a band.' She looked at him with greater interest. It was her ambition to play in a band. His expression changed and his eyes darted about as he spoke, as if he was angry.

'Lou Gaffney, fifth year student and rugby player,' Lou put in, as if he felt the need to add some qualification.

'And he has an all-Ireland medal for hurling,' added Cara.

'His sister showed it to me once.' Lou feigned embarrassment, but Ashling could see that he was pleased. And rightly so, she supposed. If she had brought as many honours to the school as Lou did, she'd feel mighty pleased too.

'And what's your name, honey?' asked Dan.

'I'm Cara and that's my sister Ashling.'

Ashling sighed as faces turned to look at her. At least Cara had saved her the cringing embarrassment of having to introduce herself.

'What about you?' Lou stuck his chin out in a superior manner as he directed his question to the young man who'd been fishing. 'What's your story?'

Everyone could see that, at first, the young man was angry. He pursed his lips and scratched his beard. His shoulders were hunched and his other hand was buried deep in the pocket of his black denim jacket. He would have been good looking were it not for his sour expression.

'None of your business,' he muttered. 'You're like a crowd at alcoholics anonymous or something. What does it matter who we are or what we are?'

'Oh, suit yourself,' said Lou, forgetting that he had been the one to scoff at introductions in the beginning.

'I will ...'

Strong light made them all shield their eyes as the door slid open and Jack Brophy's familiar bulk was silhouetted for a moment before the door closed again behind him. He made his way to the group and sat down on one of the cushions. Even in the gloom they could see that he was pale and he was twisting his hands nervously.

All at once the questions were flung at him.

'Where ..? Why ..? Who ..?'

Jack put his hands to his head. 'Wait,' he said. 'Give me a break, folks.' He looked around the anxious faces and sighed. 'I asked all those questions and I got some answers. Only some. I'll explain what I can as best I can. I was introduced to a bunch of ... of strange people on a screen - the Governing Seven they're called. A grim lot. One of them told me that these people come from a galaxy beyond ours. Their world is similar to ours, with a similar solar system, but thousands of years ahead. They went through all the stages of evolvement as our human race did, and made the same discoveries and technological advances. Their technology began to destroy their equivalent of our ozone layer, much the same as is happening here ... on earth, I mean. It got so bad that they had to resort to genetic engineering to adapt to the changing atmosphere.'

'What's that?' asked Cara.

'It means that they altered human cells so that babies would be born who could cope with the different air,' explained Ian.

'I see,' said Cara. She didn't, really, and was about to ask further questions, but she could sense the impatience of the others.

'Go on,' Ian encouraged Jack Brophy. 'What has this to do with us?'

'Well, over a couple of thousand years the genetic engineering has changed them not only physically, but emotionally as well. They know they should be warm-blooded, like us and that they should have feelings, like us. But they have become cold and indifferent. Their brains are developed way beyond anything we'll ever reach, or so they say. And their technology is light years ahead of ours.'

'I still don't understand ...' began Elizabeth.

'But their race is fading out,' continued Jack. 'They lead cold, isolated lives without physical contact. They've simply lost interest in one another as people. They realise that they are reverting back to the original inhabitants of their planet - amoebic water creatures without contact. Their babies are mostly test-tube babies and even they are not surviving very well. The scientists know that, unless they can correct this genetic trend, their world will eventually just peter out. As it is there are only about a thousand of them left.'

'That's ironic,' said Dan, as they all digested this extraordinary information. 'It seems like they've taken technology so far that the bubble has burst and now they're going backwards.'

'Something like that,' nodded Jack. 'From what I could gather - reading between the lines as it were, their whole system has broken down. They've been depending so much on computerised living that they've lost their grip on basic survival, basic living.'

'But what has this to do with us?' persisted Elizabeth. 'What do they want from us?'

Jack twisted his hands nervously again.

'I don't really know,' he said. 'One of them interrupted and said that we were chosen for our skills.'

'Our skills?' echoed Dan. 'A few adults and a handful of youngsters!'

'Yes, but some of the other Governors shouted him down in their own language so I don't know what they're at.'

'And we're still in the dark,' said Ian.

'More or less,' agreed Jack.

'More or less?'

'Well they did say why they picked Ireland,' Mr Brophy went on.

'We're one of the last pollution-free countries. We haven't been completely swamped by chemicals just yet.'

'And we're noted for our warmth and friendliness,' said Elizabeth. 'Maybe they want us to pass on some of our friendliness to them.'

'Friendly? Ha!' muttered the hostile man.

Lou looked at him with scorn. 'Yes, friendly,' he said. 'A word that wouldn't fit into your small vocabulary, mate.'

The young man scowled at him.

'But they didn't say why we in particular were chosen,' Jack ignored the interruption. 'I get the feeling that something went wrong. That things didn't quite work out for them. It's just a hunch.'

'That sounds bizarre,' said Dan. 'If you ask me, I think your man,' he nodded towards Lou, 'is right. They're going to use us as experiments. That makes more sense.'

Ashling paled at his pronouncement and felt panic rise in her throat.

'But what about the skills one of them mentioned?' Ian persisted.

'You heard the man,' said Dan. 'They shouted down the one who brought that up.'

'Look,' said Jack. 'There's no point in speculating and frightening ourselves unnecessarily,' he glanced at the scared faces of Ashling and Cara. 'Let's just stay calm and try reasoning with them when the time comes. That's all we can do.'

'There are only eight of us,' said Dan. 'Including two children and a teenage lad. Are we supposed to be the saviours of a whole race? It doesn't make sense. I think they're into something deeper, something more sinister than that.'

'It gives me the creeps just to think of it,' shuddered Ian.

'Will we be together, Jack?' Ashling's fear was evident in the shake of her voice.

Jack paused and looked at her for a moment.

'I don't know Ash,' he said. 'I wish I could say yes, but I just don't know.'

Ashling closed her eyes as if to shut out the awful dread of being separated from the others and from Cara.

The door slid open again and one of the figures placed a tray on a low shelf.

'Nourishment,' he said. 'Please take one small container and one large container each.' The door slid to again.

Nobody moved for a moment.

'Great line of chat, haven't they?' commented Dan.

'Is that food?' asked Cara angrily. Her stomach had obviously returned to normal. 'I'm hungry.' She got up and walked towards the tray. Her move prompted the others to do the same.

On the tray, in neat lines, there were plastic beakers, large and small. In the large ones a green, gel-like substance glistened in the dim light. In the smaller cups were three tablets, red, blue and yellow.

'Primary colours,' said Dan, with forced good humour as he held out a beaker to Cara. 'We're having a dinner of primary colours.'

'And snot,' said Cara, holding the green stuff up to the light. 'This stuff looks like snot.'

'I suppose it's all right,' said Elizabeth, sniffing suspiciously at the gel.

'I hardly think they're going to harm us,' said Lou. 'Not if they're depending on us for their survival.'

His remark caused Ashling's hand to shake as fear enveloped her once more. We're all in this together, she told herself. Keep calm. Everyone else is as scared as I am. But nothing would shake off the dread that shook every nerve in her body.

Four

Many hours later, or was it days - who knew what time meant any more as the group in the dim chamber alternated between anxious guessing and drugged drowsiness, Ashling looked at her watch. Was it four o'clock in the morning or afternoon? What day was it? Did days exist any more?

Something had changed - something that had roused her from her headachy sleep. She looked around at the other dozing bodies but there was no visible evidence of anything different. She gazed distractedly for a moment at Lou's outstretched figure and thought of the number of fifth year girls who would be over the moon if they were stuck up in a space ship with him. Over the moon? We really are over the moon, she snorted to herself, and it's anything but romantic.

Then she noticed; it was the hum. The hum had gone. She shook her head to make sure that it wasn't some temporary deafness. The humming sound that had buzzed through every bone in her body for so long now was replaced by eerie silence. She nudged Cara.

'Wake up,' she whispered. 'I think something is happening.'

Cara yawned noisily and stretched herself. 'Oh, Ash,' she said. 'I was dreaming that we were on the beach in Curracloe - just you and me. We were running towards an ice-cream van that kept moving away. No matter how fast we ran, it was always farther away. You know, I'd love an ice-cream ...'

'Ice-cream? I wish that was all we wanted. Listen, do you notice that the hum is gone?'

Cara cocked her ear. 'So it is,' she said. 'What does that mean, Ash?'

'I don't know. Give Lou and Jack a shake.'

Everyone was moving in the now familiar pattern of stretching after their artificially-induced sleep. Though they took turns to wash in the tiny washroom, there was still a warm, musky smell of sweat in the chamber. Clothes were creased and tatty, and the stubble on the men's faces made them look dirty. Ashling ran her fingers through her shoulder-length hair and wished she had a comb. She kept her arms tightly by her side as she made her way to the loo. She wondered had these creatures never heard of soap, as she ran the water and splashed it over her body. She never felt fully dry after using one of those automatic dryers, so she rubbed herself over with the sleeve of her cardigan.

The door of the chamber slid open wider than before. Against the light there were six or so of the creatures.

'Friggin' frog-faces,' muttered Dan.

'This way please,' one of them stepped forward and indicated that the group of prisoners should go through the open door. Nobody moved. Here, in this chamber, they had become secure together. Whatever was out there beyond that doorway would change that bond of unity. They would be exposed to the unknown and were afraid. Cara clutched Ashling's hand and Ashling drew her sister to her protectively. Still nobody moved.

'You must come this way,' the strange being's eyes flashed brighter.

'Oops, full headlights. We're in right trouble now,' muttered Dan.

Someone laughed nervously. Other creatures entered the chamber purposefully and began to usher the group towards the door.

'Ash, I don't want to go,' Cara pulled back. 'Don't let them make us go out there.'

Ashling bit her lip and looked helplessly around. Cara's fear prompted the others to action. They gathered around the child and tried to soothe her terror. The creatures were losing patience.

'Come along, move.'

Elizabeth turned haughtily and addressed the nearest one; 'Keep your hair on, sunshine. Can't you see the child is frightened?'

'There is nothing to fear,' the creature replied.

'How do we know that?' asked Ian.

'No harm will come to any of you.'

'We'd better do as they say,' said Jack. 'There's nothing to be gained from staying here. Let's take our courage in our hands and see what they have in store for us.' He went to the door and waited for the bedraggled and scared group to follow.

They were directed into a small shuttle on a single rail, which travelled very fast through a dimly lit tunnel.

'This is like Stansted Airport,' said Elizabeth.

'Maybe it is,' Dan laughed and put his hand on Cara's shoulder. Ashling could see that he was desperately trying to keep spirits up in these incredible circumstances. 'Maybe Ryanair are doing bargain spaceflights and have shifted Stansted to the skies.'

'If it was Ryanair they'd have given us soap,' said Ashling.

'And decent grub,' added Ian.

'And a cup of hot tea,' said Elizabeth wistfully.

'So I think we must agree that it's not Ryanair,' said Jack. The words were hesitant and did not hide the general air of fear, but at least they gave a communal feeling of support.

'That's stupid talk,' said Lou, casting a hostile glance at one of the guards. 'These scumbags have kidnapped us and we're stuck up here, somewhere in space, and you make jokes about Ryanair. Get real.'

'Ever heard of a sense of humour, sweetheart?' asked Elizabeth. 'It helps in times of stress, and if we lose that we slide down to depression.'

'Yeah, well a sense of humour is not going to get us out of this mess, is it? I'm all on for tackling these ugly wimps. Is there no one who'll join me?'

'To what purpose, Lou?' Jack asked patiently. 'I can fully understand your anger, but it's not like we're on familiar territory. We have no choice but to go along with them.'

Ashling looked at Lou's set chin and marvelled at his courage. Could the others not see that he was being so brave? If she were big enough and strong enough she was sure she would be thinking like Lou.

'I'd like to smash their slimy faces,' muttered Lou.

'Cut it out, son,' said Dan. 'None of this will help us.' He glanced around at the creatures who were silently observing the exchange. 'We don't want this lot to think we're some sort of primitive thugs,' he whispered.

'I don't give a ...' began Lou.

His words were cut short as the shuttle sped out of the tunnel and into the most extraordinary landscape. In a huge compound on the right trees and plants grew in abundance, arranged in neat rows, with monorail lines running through them. Small, cylindrical carriages were being loaded with various crops and then speeding towards a large building farther down the line. To the left was what appeared to be a huge industrial area. It was like a grey lego building to which someone had kept adding bits so that it appeared to be a great complex of constructions joined in places by perspex tunnels. Networks of monorails weaved through these blocks like grey spaghetti, on which three- and four-carriage shuttles sped back and forth. Myriads of pipes thrust upwards towards ...

'There's no sky!' exclaimed Cara.

Everyone peered out the window and gazed upward. Sure enough, where the sky should have been there was an enormous dome through which a diffused light cast an eerie light on the city.

'That's our Filter Dome,' said one of their escorts with a note of pride. 'That was built centuries ago when the natural filter layer became so thin that our sun's rays were beginning to burn and destroy everything on the planet. Scientists at that time devised the first Filter Dome which has saved us from extinction.'

'That's like our ozone layer!' cried Cara. 'That's happening at home, on earth. It's going all thin and things are getting burnt up. Isn't that right, Jack? Will we have to make one of these dome things as well? That's cool!'

Ashling frowned as she looked up at the multi-facetted dome. Was this what was ahead of earth? Was this our future too? She glanced at the line of creatures sitting quietly in grey similarity - their individuality lost in some past experiment of genetic engineering. She shook her head, 'Hell,' she whispered to herself. 'It would be like living in hell.'

The shuttle drew up in front of a wide entrance. Several creatures were assembled outside and they peered with interest into the shuttle as the group disembarked. Jack and Elizabeth were first out. Some of the creatures reached out and touched them. Ashling grimaced.

'If one of those things touches me I'll scream,' she whispered to Cara. 'Then I'll vomit. Yecchh.'

'I'll look after you,' said Cara, reversing the role of protectiveness. 'Stay behind me and I won't let any of them near you.'

Ashling smiled at her small sister. She knew Cara was making a huge effort to seem brave. 'Good on you, sunshine,' she said.

When they stepped out of the shuttle, the heavy, warm atmosphere made them gasp. It was like the air in Mam's hothouse - clammy and sweaty. Ashling gritted her teeth as a hand reached out and felt her hair.

'Leave my sister alone!' Cara pushed the hand away and the surprised creature retreated. Cara smiled triumphantly at Ashling. 'See. Stick with me and you'll be fine.'

They were led into the building, past groups of the creatures who regarded them with expressionless curiosity. A perspex lift took them above the ground level and enabled them to see over the stacked shoe-box arrangement of the city.

'Grey,' commented Ian. 'Did you notice that everything is grey?'

'And drab,' agreed Elizabeth. 'Have these people not discovered colour, with all their advanced technology?'

'Maybe they see everything in glorious technicolour through their orange eyes,' said Dan.

'It's a sad sort of a place, from what we've seen so far,' put in Elizabeth. 'No light, only a foggy twilight. And all these people look the same, with the same blank expressions.'

'Perhaps this IS their twilight,' said Ian. 'Perhaps we've arrived in their evening. It might get bright in the morning.'

'If there is such a thing as morning,' said Dan, drily.

'We'll just have to find out as we go along,' whispered Jack as the lift eased to a halt and their escorts held open the door.

Another walk along a shiny corridor.

'If we don't get food soon, I'll fall into a decline,' muttered Elizabeth.

'Food?' echoed Dan. 'What's that? Remind me.'

'She means those delicious tablets and the hair gel that passes for drink,' said Lou. 'Maybe they serve real food here.'

'Live in hope,' growled Dave.

'Live being the operative word,' observed Jack.

Five

'Bow in the Great Presence,' one of the escorts whispered. The confused group looked around with dismay as they were guided through double doors into a hushed chamber. The air in here was heavier and more oppressive than outside. Ashling took a sharp breath and felt like she was taking vaporized treacle into her lungs. She caught Lou's eye and he winked reassuringly. In another place at another time she'd have died at the thought of Lou Gaffney winking at her.

There was a transparent table at the far end of the large, high room. Around it sat seven dignified creatures who rose when the group entered. Their faces were not visible in the dim light which seemed to emanate from somewhere in the domed ceiling. These must be the people Mr Brophy had been speaking to.

One of them stepped forward and extended his hands.

'Welcome to Cobi,' he said, and indicated that the group should sit on the cushions arranged near the glass table. From here the faces of the seven became visible. Ashling noted with surprise that these people were different from the others. For a start they were much older and, secondly, their facial structure was nearer to human form; their noses were more pronounced and their eyes didn't glow so much.

'They look like slightly battered versions of ourselves,' whispered Dan. A sense of hope relieved the tension on the faces of the Irish captives. Perhaps now they would be shown some familiar kindness. Now they might get some answers and some sympathy. The doors behind clanged shut as the escorts departed. Ashling felt that now they were among people who would see them right.

'We are the Governing Seven,' one of them was saying. 'We must make it clear to you why we have brought you here.' He looked at the others who nodded approvingly. 'Our species is in danger. Our life form was once exactly like yours. Our world was like your world, but much has happened to change it ...'

'We know all that,' interrupted Ian, with a flash of impatience. 'But what do you really want of us? We're just ordinary people ...'

'Do not speak across the First Governor,' snapped a grey-tufted female. 'You will stay mute until we need you to speak.'

The First Governor stared coldly at Ian before continuing.

'We intended taking a large team of farmers, scientists and medical people from your country. The ship was designed to take fifty people ...'

'Fifty!' Lou whistled.

'Unfortunately,' the Governor went on, 'our ship developed trouble over the area from which you were taken. Our crew had been trained to act quickly. Because they'd landed in a remote area, it was necessary to remove whatever personnel they could without delay. Discovery was imminent - search-parties had been formed ...'

'So you're saying that you originally planned to take a lot of experts and you've ended up with a ...'

'Some of you will be of use to us,' another Governor put in.

'And the others?' asked Jack Brophy.

The Governor ignored him.

'You will live in a specially prepared compound,' he said, 'until you become acclimatised to our atmosphere. Two escorts have been assigned to stay with you and look after your needs. When you have rested, samples of your blood will be taken for analysis.'

'And after that?' Ian cut in again. 'What happens to us when we're acclimatised?'

The female made to rebuke him again, but the First Governor held up his hand. 'You will be told,' he said.

'Will we be together?' asked Elizabeth. 'We need to be together ... always ...'

'Be quiet!' another Governor had risen to his feet.

'But we need to know...' began Ian helplessly. 'You have no right to keep us here in ignorance. You must tell us ...'

Jack put out a hand to restrain Ian. 'Easy,' he whispered.

'We must tell you nothing,' said the First Governor. 'We rest.'

A steel plate slid out from the wall and encompassed the area surrounding the Governors. The captives looked at one another with frustration.

'No joy there,' said Jack.

'A right shower of gobsh ...' observed Dan

'I think we made a bit of a mess of that ourselves,' put in Elizabeth.

'I know. My fault, sorry' said Ian ruefully. 'But we'll go out of our minds if we don't get some answers. Fear of the unknown ...'

'Well, pushing them for information is certainly not going to work,' put in Lou.

'I've said I'm sorry,' began Ian.

'Easy on,' Jack held up his hand. 'We simply must stay calm, so cool it, folks.'

Ashling felt cheated. She had hoped that these dignified looking people would give them some comfort, but their hostility shattered any hopes of that. These were people to fear.

'What now, I wonder?' Elizabeth broke the awkward silence and looked expectantly around the gloomy hall.

'We must insist that we're left together,' said Ian with the logic and balance of an engineer's mind. 'I don't think any of us could handle being isolated with ...' he broke off and looked guiltily at Cara and Ashling. 'I mean, we'll make it clear to these bods that we function better as a group. We'll make sure we're all useful to them.'

Ashling felt a chill at his words.

'I'm not a child, Ian,' she said. 'I'm nearly fifteen so don't try to couch your words.' She knew she sounded braver than she felt.

Lou had gone over to the steel surround and was feeling it. Then he began to kick it. 'Open up, you pigs!' he cried. 'Open this damn shutter and talk to us.' His blows echoed around the hall. The others watched him for a moment before Ian and Dan ran to stop him. The bearded young man, who had finally revealed that his name$was Dave, looked on with hunched shoulders and a scowl.

'Leave it, lad,' said Dan. 'No point in making them angry.'

'Angry?' Lou broke from their restraining grip and began kicking the steel plate again. 'I'll show them angry.'

'That lad will ruin any hope we have,' said Elizabeth. 'Stop, Lou! Have a bit of sense, for crying out loud!'

But Lou continued to kick. He was working himself up to a fury which was frightening. Ashling moved closer to Cara. This was a familiar, human anger but, somehow, it seemed much more terrifying in this awful place. She could feel her own panic rising. Please don't let me lose control. She clutched Cara to make her protectiveness overcome the panic.

Three creatures appeared from a door in the side wall. They ran across to where Lou was shouting. One of them simply put a hand to Lou's neck and he collapsed like a rag doll.

'That's neat,' said Cara, who was totally unmoved by the fuss. 'I wonder if he'd teach me to do that. I could beat up that Barry O'Keefe. He's a big bully ...' she stopped when she realised that Barry O'Keefe was light years away and wished, more than anything, that Barry O'Keefe was the only problem right now. She looked up at Ashling's tense face and was glad her sister was with her. The creatures picked up Lou and carried him with ease. They beckoned to the others to follow.

'Now where?' sighed Elizabeth.

'Just follow the Yellow Brick Road,' Dan muttered. 'We're off to see the Wizard, the wonderful Wizard of Oz.'

'Oh, Dan. I'm beyond responding to jokes,' Elizabeth gave him a weary smile. 'If I don't get a breath of air soon, I'll smother.'

After traipsing the length of yet another long passageway, they were ushered into a large area which was divided into a complex of smaller quarters. The air here was cooler and less oppressive. There were bunks and sofas and easy chairs. On a table there was a jug and beakers. Clothes, similar to the ones their captors were wearing, were laid out on the bunks.

'Grey, of course,' observed Ian.

'You may change into these,' said one of their escorts.

'Not me,' said Dan, clutching his blue sweater. 'These threads are my only link with home; damned if I'll part with them.'

'Me neither,' said Elizabeth, whose hand went to the small cross pinned to her navy jumper.

'I think those suits are groovy,' said Cara, already taking off her sweatshirt. 'Sugar! This one's too big,' her muffled voice came from inside the one-piece outfit.

'They all look the same size,' Elizabeth pointed out. 'I don't really fancy one, though if it's all the same with you.' She turned to the Cobians who were standing apart, watching. 'I'll hang on to my own comfy togs.'

'You will change ... now,' one of them stepped forward. 'That fabric you all wear causes dust which we cannot tolerate.'

'Better do as he says,' said Jack resignedly. 'No point in causing more trouble. We'd also better allocate where we're going to sleep. Since they've dumped Lou here, I suppose we men will take the bunks on this side. We'll toss for who goes up or down.'

One of the escorts followed Elizabeth and Ashling across the room.

Elizabeth was holding Cara's hand, a gesture which gave

Ashling some comfort.

'Excuse us,' said Elizabeth. 'We'd like a bit of privacy, if you don't mind, honeybun. Push off,' and she pulled the movable screen firmly across. The creature shrugged his shoulders and retreated.

'Actually these suits feel nice,' observed Ashling. 'They're silky without being cold.'

'So they are,' said Elizabeth. 'Very comfortable. Listen to us. We sound like an ad for washing powder.'

'That's a nice brooch,' said Ashling, peering closer to look at Elizabeth's collar.

'It's the silver brooch of our order,' Elizabeth shone the brooch on her sleeve.

'Order?' Ashling asked. 'Are you ..?'

'A nun. Yes, Holy Family.' Elizabeth was putting a light cover over the sleepy Cara who was curled up on a top bunk. 'Can't think what this lot would want with a nun. There I was, enjoying a nice break after eight years in the Third World and I end up out of the world.'

'What were you doing there, in the Third World, I mean?' Ashling felt she had to keep talking, because, if conversation stopped, the waves of panic she'd been holding back would probably overcome her and she'd go ber ... berserk.

'At first I was in Ethiopia, during that awful famine,' Elizabeth was saying. She paused for a moment, as if lost in memory. Then she sighed.

'More recently I was in Rwanda,' she said. 'Nothing, either in our world or this, could possibly equal the horror and pain of that place.' She frowned slightly and shook her head. 'I felt so bad about having to leave,' she went on. 'About having to flee from the very people I'd been teaching basic survival to ...' she lapsed into silence again. Then, as if she suddenly remembered that Ashling was there, she smiled. 'That's all in the past. What we've got to do is make sure that we all survive this ... this bizarre situation. Try not to worry, dear. We must all stand by one another.'

Ashling nodded as she curled up on the upper bunk. Not worry! She tried to keep her thoughts from wandering into the depths of panic. Fortunately, exhaustion intervened and she slipped into a deep sleep.

Six

When Ashling awoke, she felt that the colouring should have changed from the dull grey of twilight to the glow of morning. She was disappointed; the same drabness surrounded her. It was like constantly waking up from a bad dream only to find yourself back in it again. The fact that there was no change in the light was disconcerting. It gave no focal point to time and made her feel sick and sluggish. That, mixed with the deep-seated fear of what might lie ahead for all of them made her want to sleep again - to be unconscious would remove the dread.

She half-smiled when she heard Cara's voice from across the room. She sounded so normal as she explored the strange room.

'Get a load of this weird place,' she called to her sister. 'It's like seeing Star Trek from the inside.' Then she sighed as realisation dawned on her. 'I wish it was just Star Trek. I wish ...' her voice trailed off.

Now everyone was stirring. The two escorts came silently through the sliding doors as if on cue. One of them carried a tray with the now familiar jug of gunge and pile of pills.

'Oh, breakfast,' said Dan, zipping up his new outfit. 'How do you like your snot, Miss, poached or fried?' he asked Cara, who giggled.

'He's a good sort, that Dan,' observed Elizabeth, struggling into her suit. Ashling noticed that she had freckles on her chest and wondered if she wore her habit in the Third World. The Third World, she pondered. With all its wars and famines she would prefer to be there than in this unreal place.

'Human nature is amazing,' continued Elizabeth. 'When you think of the most horrendous disasters and catastrophes, it's extraordinary how people will adapt and make the most of situations. The thing is,' her voice was muffled as she dressed. 'The thing is not to crack up.'

As Ashling listened she felt the cold fear rise up the back of her neck again. What if she was the one who did crack up? What if that panicky feeling deep in her stomach took over and she went mad with terror? She took a deep breath, like her mother told her to do whenever she felt under pressure. But this air was heavy and headachy and she didn't want to think of her mother anyway. If she did, she would revert to childish emotions, and there was no time for that. She gave a shallow sigh and went to join the others.

'Do you think they might give us some soap?' she asked Elizabeth, hoping that sticking to ordinary topics would reduce the grotesque horror of this place.

'Ask old frogface there,' said Elizabeth.

'Soap?' said the Cobian in response to Ashling's request. 'We don't use that. Soap went out of production a long time ago. It does not agree with our skin.'

'But what do you clean yourselves with?'

'We have no need to clean ourselves. Dirt and grime and dust have been eliminated.'

'Well, so much for hygiene,' said Elizabeth drily. 'Do you at least have water so that we can freshen up?'

The Cobian indicated another door.

'Another superloo, I'll bet,' said Cara. And it was, Ashling noted with relief. It had running warm water, and towels of some sort of silky stuff had been left out for the group. At least her hair looked better than it had done.

When they had eaten, they were taken to a laboratory-type place where several Cobians awaited them.

'What are they going to do?' asked Cara nervously.

'They said that they were just going to take blood

samples,' said Ian. 'They're not going to do us any harm.'

'I don't like this,' Cara's voice had raised a pitch. 'I don't want to go in there.'

'It's all right, sweetheart,' soothed Dan. 'You don't think they've brought us all this way to do something threatening to us, do you?'

But Cara was not convinced.

'Ash,' she said. 'Tell them to leave us alone ...'

But two of the Cobians stepped forward and swept the child on to a table, ignoring her hysterical cries and strapping her down.

'Wait a moment,' called Ian, reaching towards Cara. His thin face was white with barely concealed temper. 'Can't you see the youngster is frightened?'

'Leave her alone,' pleaded Ashling. 'At least let me sit with her.'

The others also raised their voices to protest at the treatment of the scared Cara. But these creatures knew what they were at and heeded no one. Each of the group was strapped to a table. Ashling wished she could faint. The creatures went about their business coldly and silently against the panicky cries of Cara.

'It's all right,' called Elizabeth. 'I know what they're doing. They really are only taking blood. Just relax. Believe me, it's OK.'

Ashling watched with fearful fascination as her blood flowed through a tube into a clear container. It was all over in moments and they were ushered back to their quarters.

'What a cold lot those Cobians are,' said Elizabeth, sitting into one of the moulded easy-chairs. 'They could at least have tried to calm the child instead of grabbing her like that. They could have explained what a simple exercise it was and put her mind at ease.' She put her arm around Cara. But Cara, ashamed of her outburst, shrugged her off. 'I'm all right,' she muttered. She wished they'd all forget and not make a fuss of her.

'Let's just remember that these people have no emotions,' said Jack. 'We know now that they won't respond to pleas and cries. They are cold-blooded reptiles. We're up against more than just physical force; they don't care tuppence for us. At least we know where we stand.'

His words cast a chill silence on everyone.

They sat around listlessly in their quarters, each seemingly lost in a private fear. The morning's event had served only to stamp the realisation that this was real and fearsome. The camaraderie they'd built up together was a fragile thing easily shattered by the cold Cobians in their search for their own survival.

Cara, her ordeal forgotten, stared at one of the escorts with childish curiosity. The other one had left.

'What's your name?' she asked at length.

The creature looked down at the small girl and it seemed he was going to ignore her. He looked about as if not knowing quite how to handle the situation.

'I don't have a name,' he said.

'That's silly,' said Cara. 'If you have no name how can you talk to one another?'

'When we reach maturity we are given functional titles,' explained the Cobian. 'Each of us has a function for which we are trained from infancy. That function then becomes our title.'

'And what's your function?'

'I have been trained to study your planet and its people. For a very long time I have monitored humans as they exist now, and, on our vast computers, I have studied the development of your people from the beginning.'

'I bet you don't know everything,' said Cara. 'You'd have to be like us to know us. I bet there's loads you don't know.'

The others listened in silence to the exchange between the child and the tall Cobian.

'We were like you, once,' continued the Cobian.

'And what happened?' asked Cara frankly. 'How come you've gone all squashy-faced and ... and ugly? Will you ever get better?'

The Cobian made a funny noise.

Oh, lord, thought Ashling, Cara's upset him. She glanced at the anxious faces of the others and knew they were thinking the same. The sound turned into a sort of cackle. She looked fearfully across at him. The creature was laughing! His mouth had broadened to reveal tiny, sharp teeth and his eyes were crinkled in an expression of mirth.

Cara was oblivious to the relieved listeners behind her and continued to focus her attention on the Cobian.

'So, what's your title, anyway?'

'I'm referred to as Earth Monitor Four.'

Cara digested this information for a moment, then she grinned.

'That's an awful mouthful,' she said. 'Does your mother say "Would you like more cake, Earth Monitor Four?" or does your girlfriend say "Give us a kiss, Earth Monitor Four"?'

The Cobian smiled as he answered. 'We don't have cake and we don't have girlfriends,' he said simply. 'And we don't have mothers.'

'You're very strange,' said Cara. 'Anyway, I'll call you a name. Let me see .... You remind me of a goldfish my granny had. It was called Toby because Granny really wanted a dog but they wouldn't let her have one in the flat. I'll call you Toby.'

'I'm to be called after a goldfish and a dog?' the Cobian smiled again.

'Well, isn't it better than Earth Monitor Four? Anyway, it's nice to be called after friendly things. So, tell me, Toby,' Cara sat on the step and made herself comfortable. 'How come you speak our language? It's pretty weird, you come from another planet and you can speak English. Although you do speak it in a funny way - like in old-fashioned films.'

Toby sat down beside Cara and stretched out his long legs.

'Like I told you, a number of us were trained to study all things earthly, including the major languages. If you were

French or German I would also be able to converse with you.'

The group listened unashamedly to the conversation. Perhaps it was within the power of a small girl to break down the cold reserve of these alien beings.

'Why didn't you take some people from there, then? Jack Brophy says it's because Ireland has no pollution, is that right?'

Toby nodded. 'One of the few countries left with no pollution,' he agreed. 'And also, your people are warmer ...'

'Warmer? You must be joking,' exclaimed Cara. 'Our climate is cold and wet ...'

'I don't mean climate,' put in Toby. 'I mean your people care for one another better than most. That's what other countries are losing and what we've lost altogether. That warmth that keeps people functioning together. That's one of the reasons we chose Ireland. Sometimes, in science, it's the simplest formula that can lead to the right answers.'

'I see,' began Cara. 'I think I see.' She looked intently into the Cobian's face. 'What do you want our blood for? Are you going to experiment with us?'

Toby hesitated before answering. 'For cloning purposes,' he said. 'To see if we can clone some ...' A bleeper sounded from somewhere and his face froze back to its original cold expression. 'I must go,' he said, rising.

Cara wandered back to the others.

'What's cloning?' she asked.

'It means that they can take a little bit of our blood and make more blood from it,' said Dan. He looked at the others. 'I suppose it makes some sense,' he continued, half questioningly.

'I suppose so,' said Jack. 'If they can manufacture enough blood to pass on, through transfusion, to the rest of their gang, it might have an effect on their survival.'

'If it stops at just taking blood,' said Ian ominously.

'You've said it,' sighed Jack. 'It seems too simple a matter to haul a handful of us up from earth just to take a few pints of blood. If that's all they wanted, they could have nipped into any blood bank and helped themselves.'

The others nodded in agreement.

'Maybe it is all they want,' said Dan hopefully.

Elizabeth shook her head. 'It wouldn't stop there,' she said. 'Think about it. Their technology is so far advanced that they could clone anything - so long as they had the original to clone from.'

'What do you mean?' asked Ashling. This conversation was frightening her. Part of her wanted to know everything - to have all the possibilities explained to her. Another part of her wanted to curl up and hear nothing of what the adults were talking about. But she knew if she did that, her imagination would conjure up images far more frightening than the reality.

Elizabeth looked at her doubtfully, as if she'd prefer not to have to spell out, in so many words, just what might lie ahead of them. She then glanced at Cara.

'It's OK,' said Jack gently. 'We're all in this together. It's important that we all know where we stand and what to ... to look out for.'

'He's right,' said Dan. '

They huddled closer together to listen to what Elizabeth was saying.

Elizabeth looked again at Ashling and Cara, wondering how best to voice her fears without frightening the two of them too much.

'It's like making a photocopy,' she said. 'You know how you have to have an original to put into the machine before you can make a copy of it?'

'So they're going to sort of photocopy our blood?' asked Cara. That didn't sound too bad.

But Ashling looked at the faces of the others and knew that cloning had a deeper meaning. She racked her brains to try and remember how cloning had been explained in science class. Why didn't she pay more attention instead of drawing guitarists with tattoos in her science book? Couldn't cloning be used to reproduce organs like hearts and kidneys and things?

'Organs,' she said to Elizabeth. 'You're talking about organs, aren't you?'

'I am. Organs and, probably, brain tissue.'

They all let that sink in for a moment. Ashling shivered slightly. A deep despair took hold of her and she moved closer to Jack.

'It doesn't mean that they'll do us in to get all these bits and pieces, does it?' Dan tried to sound cheerful. 'There's no reason why we can't all afford little bits of ... of tissue, is there?'

Elizabeth fidgeted with her fingers before replying. 'No reason at all,' she said. But the way she said it didn't convince Ashling.

Seven

'How long must we go on like this?' asked Elizabeth. 'These walls are beginning to close in on me. I think I'm getting claustrophobia.'

'Join us in our exercise,' said Ian, who had organised a fitness routine. 'If we keep active we'll stay on top of captivity.'

'Sod the exercise,' retorted Elizabeth in a very un-nunlike manner. 'All I want is to get out of this room before I get the screaming mimis.' She glanced across at the other escort whose turn it was to supervise the group. He had responded in no way to friendly overtures, remaining cold and silently aloof. Dan had christened him 'Scud' because, 'He looks the type who'd spit Scud missiles at you,' Dan had said.

'What about it, Scud?' Elizabeth called out. 'Any chance you'd take us on a walkabout?' But Scud's only response was to stare fixedly ahead.

'He's not programmed to respond to nuns,' panted Dan between press-ups.

But, to their surprise, they were taken out later that day. Both Toby and Scud ushered them back the way they had come, how long ago now? They had forgotten how oppressive the air had been when they'd arrived. They gasped as the warm, syrupy atmosphere gagged the backs of their throats. After a while they got used to taking short, shallow breaths. The stacked shoe-box arrangement of buildings seemed quite vast when viewed from this angle. Shuttles whirred quietly along the network of monorails.

There weren't many people about outdoors, and those who were, were busily engaged in offloading big boxes from cargo shuttles.

'Our nourishment,' explained Toby. He pointed to the factory-type building in the distance which the group had seen on their way into the city. 'Those crops which you see are converted into all the nutrients necessary for life.'

'You mean all that greenery is just mushed up and made into pills?' asked Dan, with his cook's curiosity.

Toby nodded. 'And liquid.'

'Don't you ever consider just eating the crops as they are?' said Dan.

Toby smiled. 'That would be very inconvenient,' he said.

'But eating is one of life's great pleasures,' put in Elizabeth. 'Don't you ever want to sit down to a nice hot meal and a glass of wine?'

'I believe there was a time when that was done,' said Toby. 'But that was long ago.'

Dan sighed. 'What I'd give to get my hands on some of those crops in their natural state,' he said.

'Don't let's talk about food,' said Ian, patting his stomach. 'You'll have us drooling.'

Their journey took them around a complete circuit of the city. As they rounded the final bend they could see a compound to the left. In it were parked a couple of space craft and two lines of shuttle type vehicles behind a complex of fencing.

'That's the one you came in,' Toby pointed to a small spaceship which was being worked on by a team of mechanics.

The group fell silent as they gazed at the object which had taken them so far from home. Ashling jumped as Lou laid his hand on her shoulder. It felt nice. She hoped he wouldn't notice that her pulse was beating faster. There had been nights when she'd look at her reflection in the mirror and imagine someone like Lou Gaffney touching her. Now it was happening and she didn't know how to respond.

If we could just drive that thing,' he whispered, pointing towards the space craft.

Ashling swallowed back her confusion and nodded. She was afraid if she spoke, her voice would come out as a squeak.

Scud said something in his own language to Toby and they began to argue.

'How come Toby is so different?' asked Cara, watching the exchange.

'Probably because he's spent most of his life studying us,' said Jack.

Cara stood on her toes and peered over the balcony wall at a yellow wasteland that stretched into a misty nothingness.

'What's that?' she asked.

'It's called Deadland,' said Toby, moving away from Scud. 'Nothing survives there; it is outside the Atmosphere Ring.'

Ashling shuddered as she looked at the parched, yellow surface. It reminded her of the lifeless skin that stretched across her granny's forehead when she died. Death, death, everything in this place smacked of death. She glanced at Jack and saw him looking intently at the barren land. The confident set of his jaw should have given her some comfort, but she was too weary to reach out for any hope. Nothing could give any consolation in this dreary place so far from home.

Having had freedom of movement for however short a time made the quarters seem even smaller than before. The group were tired from the effort of walking with such limited air, and they collapsed on to their bunks. Elizabeth and Ashling curled up on Elizabeth's bunk. Above them, Cara was sprawled face downwards on her own bed. Ashling envied her little sister's ability to fall into the soothing oblivion of sleep.

Elizabeth rubbed her face with her hands as if to get the circulation going again.

'What a drab place this is,' she said. 'We've walked all

around the city and hardly saw anybody. No shops, no lights, no music. What do people do all day?'

'Well, we were only around the outer part,' said Ian from the centre of the room. 'Perhaps the rest are inside having a high old time.'

'Some hope,' mused Elizabeth. 'Seems to me their only concern is survival. Who'd want to survive in such misery..?' She stopped when she realised what she'd said.

Nobody referred to the cloning issue again and Ashling wondered if Elizabeth's simple explanation was right - perhaps the Cobians were only going to clone small amounts of blood. Would they have taken the group on a tour today if they were simply going to kill them for their organs? That wouldn't make sense. She tried to hold on to this thought and pushed her fears to the back of her mind. There they rested like a temporarily eased toothache.

Later on Toby arrived with something wrapped in a bundle. He opened it out on the table. The others gasped. It was a pile of limp looking vegetables, a bottle of clear liquid, some strange looking eggs and a knife.

'Is that food, Toby?' asked Ian.

Toby nodded. 'Untreated crops,' he said.

'Toby, you genius,' exclaimed Ian. 'Dan, you're the food expert. What are these?'

Dan sniffed at the odd-looking crop. 'These greens are a sort of lettuce,' he said. 'And I think that these yellow things were once tomatoes in a previous existence. Near enough, anyway.' He sniffed at the bottle. 'Vinegar,' he announced. 'It's just vinegar. This is great. We have the makings of a tossed salad here. If we had a big bowl I could turn out a feast.'

The exercise of putting together a primitive salad dish put the confined group into high spirits.

'Toby,' said Cara. 'Come over and see what real food tastes like. See what you're missing.'

Ashling nudged her sister. 'Look at you, getting excited about veggies and at home all you'd eat were burgers and fish fingers.'

The simple meal generated an atmosphere of festivity. Even Dave's hostility was submerged in the good vibes. At least he sat with them and seemed to enjoy the food. For a short while they all forgot the circumstances which had them where they were.

'This is like a party,' said Dan, pushing the last of the salad towards Elizabeth. 'If we had a piano now we could dance. Don't suppose you have a piano or guitar about your person, Toby?' he asked.

Toby smiled. He had watched, fascinated, as his charges ate the untreated nourishment but, in spite of their invitation, he couldn't bring himself to taste it.

'I can play the spoons,' said Ian, grabbing two of the steel spoons from the table. He rapped them against his knee and made a sort of rhythm. Jack grabbed Elizabeth and danced her around the small floor. Ashling looked at Lou. Part of her wanted him to ask her to dance. But another part of her knew that, if he did, she would be all feet and elbows, stumbling about.

She'd once seen Lou ask out Mattie O'Brien at a school disco. Everyone knew that he did it for a dare; Mattie was a shadowy loner of a girl. She wore bottle-end glasses which she was constantly pushing nervously along her thin nose. She wore dresses that her mother made and didn't seem to notice that they were gross. Nobody said much to Mattie.

Her face had lit up when Lou Gaffney called her into his head-bang group. It was a disaster. Poor Mattie got the rhythm all wrong and looked ridiculous. Then, when Lou swept her into a slow dance, she'd stumbled blushingly against him as they moved. Lou made faces over her shoulder. When it was over, Lou's pals had given him a cheer and fell about laughing. Everyone said what a right naf he was, asking Mattie O'Brien to dance. He loudly enjoyed their teasing.

Ashling recalled Mattie's face as all the joy drained from it. Why should she remember Mattie O'Brien now? Maybe circumstances were giving her a different set of values, she mused. There was more to life than superficial popularity.

Still, Lou was a cool dude, a fine hunk.

He caught her looking at him and he nodded towards the dancers. Then he held out his hand. Ashling blushed. She looked at the proffered hand and realised that this was a Mattie O'Brien situation, that he expected her to be grateful for asking her.

She shook her head. 'No,' she mouthed. At first Lou looked puzzled. Then he shrugged his shoulders in a dismissive gesture. Ashling put her hands to her warm face and wondered if she'd really done that. Was she losing her marbles? Why was she always doing the wrong thing?

The others had taken to the floor and Cara was teaching Toby to head-bang. Across the room, Dave had retired to his usual corner with the usual resentful expression on his face.

'Come on, Ashling,' called Jack. 'Join the dance.'

Ashling grimaced, glancing at Lou who was now doing press-ups. I certainly won't be dragged in like some little girl to play with the adults, she thought. Nor am I going to sit here looking like a miserable little snot. She got up and went across to Dave.

'Hi,' she said, sitting beside him.

He looked at her with surprise and moved over. 'Hi.' There was an awkward pause and Ashling realised that she would have to do the talking. From one mess to another.

'Nice to see them having a bit of fun,' she said.

Dave grunted.

'Well it's certainly better than giving in to our fears,' Ashling wondered if she should, after all, swallow her pride and take to the floor. Show both Cara and Toby some REAL head-banging.

'Won't do no good, though,' Dave's words spilled out in a rush.

'What do you mean?'

'All that false jollity. It won't get us anywhere. We're doomed in this place. Things will change and we don't know where we'll end up. They're only acting the fool, them. It's stupid what they're at.'

Ashling looked at the laughing dancers as they boisterously weaved about the alien room and felt an overwhelming loyalty.

'That's what has brought people through wars and things,' she said, 'If you read about the Jews in the most awful death camps, they even clutched on to anything that would help them forget their conditions for a moment. It's our human nature ...'

'Don't read books, me,' said Dave, fiddling with his too-long sleeve and revealing a crudely executed tattoo of an eagle.

'That's nice,' said Ashling, changing the subject. Dave ran his finger along the heavy line of the home-made tattoo.

'Had it done inside,' he said.

'Inside where?'

He looked at her with a mixture of defiance and contempt. 'In the slammer.'

If he thinks he's going to shock me, he can think again, thought Ashling.

'What were you in for?'

'GBH. Grievous bodily harm,' he said grimly.

'You mean you beat somebody up?' now she really was shocked.

'Yeah.'

'Well, I suppose you had your reasons,' she said lamely. Dave simply smiled bitterly and shook his head. 'What were you doing in our part of the country that you got caught up in this?' she continued.

'Skipping parole. Should have stayed put.' He pulled his sleeve down over his tattoo and pressed his fist into the palm of his other hand.

'You're a very angry person,' Ashling said frankly. 'That's an awful waste of time. Being angry, I mean.'

'There's not much to feel good about,' he retorted. 'See that lot out there?' he nodded towards the dancers. 'That lot wouldn't bid the likes of me the time of day at home.

People like them think people like me are the scum of the earth. And you,' he turned to look at Ashling. 'You would never sit and talk to me ...'

Ashling, who went to a very mixed community school, felt irritated.

'That's crap,' she snorted. 'I know your type. You feel the whole world is out to get you - everyone else is at fault because you can't get your act together, so you work up a hatred like ... like a brick wall around your head and spit at the rest of the world.'

'Ha, just you try standing in a dole queue with some snotty-nosed civil servant looking at you as if you were something they'd stepped in. That's not the stuff of good cheer.'

'Well, of course it's not,' Ashling agreed. 'But there are thousands on the dole queue. They don't all go around full of hate ...'

'So, what would you do?' Dave cut in.

Ashling shrugged her shoulders. 'I don't really know. But what I do know is that I wouldn't suddenly switch off from the human race.'

'Yeah, well you don't know until you find yourself in that position, so don't preach to me, lady.'

'And you don't know what people are like unless you let them through to you. You might just be surprised, Mr Crabface, that there are people who care about others.' She got up in a fury and went defiantly to where Cara and Toby were still trying to master head-banging.

Later on, when Toby was replaced by Scud, the short-lived fun had worn off and everyone was reminded of how far they were from home where such things were normal.

'We still don't know which is day and which is night,' said Elizabeth. 'I suppose we might as well retire.'

Coming back from washing, someone touched Ashling's arm. It was Dave.

'It wasn't my fault,' he said.

'What?'

'The GBH. It wasn't my fault. I thumped a drunken

driver who ran over my sister's kid and got away with a stupid fine. Judge didn't see it my way and I got done. Just thought you'd like to know.'

Ashling smiled at him. 'Thanks,' she said. 'Thanks for telling me.'

Eight

What seemed to be a small army of Cobians clattered into the room after the long sleep. The earth group were barely given time to dress before being shunted outside. Ashling suppressed a scream when she saw that they were being separated. She watched helplessly as Cara was dragged, shouting, away from her.

'Leave her with me,' she shouted, shrugging off the restraining hand of a Cobian. 'She's frightened ...'

But two of the guards simply pulled her along a narrow corridor. This was what she had dreaded most of all - being alone with these creatures. She felt the blood drain from her face as she was ushered into a laboratory-type room and hoisted into a recliner. As she struggled, her arms and legs were strapped tightly.

'Let me go, you slimy creeps!' she shouted. The Cobians ignored her insults and coldly went about their business, checking monitor screens and turning knobs on a huge console on the wall.

'Please,' she changed her tone from anger to pleading. 'Please let me go.' She glanced wildly around the terrifying place, not quite believing that all this was really happening. It was as if part of her was detached, watching something that had nothing to do with her. But deep inside an unfathomable fear caused every nerve to tremble. She screamed and shook her head as a long needle was thrust into her arm. This was much different from the blood test they'd all had recently.

'What are you doing?' she shouted. 'Let me go. I'll ... I'll die and then I won't be of any use to you.' But she was wasting her breath. She screamed again as a large helmet was thrust over her head, shutting her into a ghastly, claustrophobic darkness. She fought for breath as the cold metal seemed to block off the air. A humming noise grew to a piercing wail and lights exploded in her head. 'Please let me die,' she tried to say, just before she blacked out.

When she came to she was back among the others. Elizabeth was bathing her face with warm water.

'Elizabeth. Thank God it's you,' she mumbled with relief.

'You're all right, honeybun,' said Elizabeth. 'We're nearly all back together again. Take it easy.'

Another face came into focus. It was Dan.

'OK kid?' he smiled.

Ashling flexed her muscles and felt a stiffness in her left arm. There was a thin dressing on her mid-forearm.

'What do you think this is?' she asked.

Elizabeth gently raised part of the dressing and peered underneath.

'There seems to be a tiny bit of skin gone,' she said. 'Obviously some sort of skin test. Where were you, do you know?'

Ashling told them about the laboratory and the helmet.

'What about you?' she asked. 'Where were you?'

Elizabeth's face became tense. She hesitated before answering.

'They took me to their clinic,' she said. 'There's a lot of very ill ... people there.'

'What's wrong with them?' asked Dan.

'Their blood has thinned to the point of uselessness. And their skin ...' she paused and glanced at Ashling.

'What about their skin?' Ashling was almost afraid to ask.

'Their skin has peeled away to the extent of allowing all sorts of infection - even in these sterile conditions. They're all doomed to die.' She shook her head.

'I suppose that explains why they did a skin test on me,' Ashling was surprised at how calm she was. 'They're probably going to try skin grafts or something. Did they do skin tests on anyone else?' She tried to raise her head to look at the others, but the dull ache caused her to lie down again, but not before she saw the anxious glance that passed between Dan and Elizabeth. She felt the panic rise in her throat again.

'It was just me, was it?'

'Look, stop worrying about it,' said Dan. 'So, they took a skin test. It doesn't mean anything. They're not going to harm any of us. They need us, remember that.'

'Cara ..?' began Ashling.

Dan nodded towards the centre of the room.

'Not a bother on her,' he grinned.

The others were talking now, telling where they'd been. At least being split up gave them something to talk about now. Dan had been taken across to the food processing plant (and had succeeded in bringing back some more untreated vegetables).

'I don't know how they survive on the poor quality crops they grow,' he said. 'They have to add artificial nutrients to them. Everything is dehydrated, pressed and treated with chemicals. No meat. It's all fruit and veg. They do have poultry, of sorts. But they're only for laying these tiny eggs. When they're old, they're killed and cremated. The ashes are used as fertiliser. They've never heard of chicken soup.'

'Have they fish?' asked Elizabeth.

'No. Seems their seas rejected all living things centuries ago. There's no such thing as fish. Weird.'

'What about you, Dave?' asked Ashling. Elizabeth had helped her over to a reclining chair. Her head was feeling less achy. 'Where were you?'

Dave looked at his hands and seemed to be embarrassed.

'Tests,' he said. 'They did tests. On my head.'

'See, Ashling?' Elizabeth said. 'You weren't the only one subjected to tests.'

Ashling knew she should have felt better, but she didn't. She couldn't get those evil-looking Cobians out of her mind as they'd ignored her fears with complete indifference.

'I was in a sort of school,' put in Cara. She poked curiously at the dressing on her sister's arm. 'There were four others about my age. They were looking at computer screens, but there were no games on them. It was all numbers and stuff. Boring. I don't want to go there again. They measured me and looked at the colour of my eyes and all sorts of weird stuff. The only interesting thing was when they put a picture of me on the screen. They kept pressing buttons and parts of my picture changed colours.'

Ashling glanced at Elizabeth and noted the flash of anxiety on her face at Cara's words.

'What about you?' Elizabeth asked Jack. 'Where were you?'

'They took me to their historical research module,' he said. 'That's what they call it. You know, they really did look quite like us. It was like looking at old friends, seeing their reconstructions of the earlier species. Made me homesick. Sorry. I shouldn't have said that.'

'And what happened in their evolution that turned them into ... into these lizards?' asked Dan. 'Did you find out any more than we already know?'

Jack shook his head. 'Just that they developed an allergy to their own atmosphere. Before the dome was erected, they were dying like flies from simple things like dust and heat.' He paused and rested his face in his hands. 'Some of their genetic engineering went very wrong,' he continued in an undertone. 'There are pictures of creatures down there who look like ... like some grotesque extras in a horror movie.'

The others looked at him in silence. 'There's a tank with two big seal-like creatures ...' he shook his head again. 'It's sick to think what they've done to living things in their efforts to find their own survival.' He broke off, lost in the memory of what he'd just seen.

'Well, it's encouraging to know that we've been taken to places that relate to what we each do,' Dan tried to banish the heavy cloud that had settled over the group. 'At least it might mean that they do want our help in some way.'

Jack smiled wryly. 'I'm just a farmer, Dan. Can't think why they're showing me their ... mistakes.'

'Probably need to get back to using the land properly,' volunteered Elizabeth. 'After all farming is nearly as old as mankind. If the land is used properly, people survive. Seems to me that you and Dan are the most important ones in our group. You can restore these people to basic survival ...'

'You see!' Ashling cried. 'You've all got some skill that they're interested in. Cara and me and ... and Dave, we don't have anything to offer except ... except.'

'Except what, Ashling?' Cara looked anxiously at her sister. 'What are you saying?'

'Spare parts!' she exclaimed.

'What?' Elizabeth and Dan spoke together.

'They're going to use us - the ones with no skills - for spare parts like skin and things. For the cloning you were talking about. I'm sure of it. What else would they use us for? Don't you see? I feel it. I feel the only use we will be is to provide our bodies. The rest of you have all got some sort of skill. They need you for that, but they don't need ...'

'Us?' Cara was getting hysterical. 'They don't need us?'

Ashling bit her lip. Why couldn't she have kept her big mouth shut?

'I didn't mean anything, really,' She said lamely. 'Honest, Cara, I was just rambling. Forget it.'

'She was talking through her hat,' said Jack, and he glared at Ashling over Cara's head. She blushed and felt a fool. At almost fifteen she should have been beyond such a childish outburst, all she'd succeeded in doing was scaring her kid sister. At least Lou wasn't here to see her childish display of fear. Lou wouldn't have done that. Lou would act in anger, but never cringe like she'd just done. What about Lou? What had he to offer the Cobians? Well, he's brilliant at games and physical things. That's it - he'd train the Cobians to be fit. There, she was right, the only misplaced people were herself, Cara and Dave.

'Where are Lou and Ian?' asked Dan, as if he'd read her mind. 'Haven't they come back yet?'

They looked towards the bunks, but there was no sign of either.

'Wonder why they're keeping them longer,' said Elizabeth, trying to keep the concern out of her voice. Just then, on cue, the door slid open and Lou was half carried in by Toby and another Cobian.

'What's happened?' asked Jack, rushing to Lou. Toby pushed him away gently.

'He's all right,' he said. 'A bit tired, that's all ...'

'Tired?' Jack said. 'His face is bruised and there are marks on his neck.'

Toby shook his head. 'They shouldn't have tried to burst into places where they were not supposed to go,' he said. 'It had happened before I got there. I'm really sorry. Please, trust me when I tell you to obey the rules. My people don't understand like I do.'

'What do you mean?' asked Jack.

'They tried to break into the Great Presence,' said Toby. 'I can't think what they hoped to achieve. I ... I managed to get there before the guards shut the Expulsion Cylinder on this one.'

A deathly silence fell on the group. It was as if each one was too frightened of the answer they might get to the obvious question. It was Cara who broke the awful quiet.

'What cylinder?' she asked. 'What are you talking about, Toby?'

Toby seemed to sigh before answering. He didn't look at Cara, but at Jack. 'The Expulsion Cylinder is used to project those guilty of misdemeanours into the Outer Beyond. It was lucky I arrived when I did. I promised that none of you would try anything again ...'

'And Ian?' put in Dan. 'Where's Ian?'

Toby made a helpless gesture with his hands. 'I'm afraid I was late for Ian,' he said.

'You mean ..?'

'He had already been expelled.'

'The animals,' said Jack, for once losing his calm demeanour. 'The cold-blooded animals.'

'I'm really sorry,' said Toby. 'If only I had known what they were going to do, I could have prevented all this. You don't know how sorry I am. The Governing Seven are angry. There's nothing I can do now,' he added cryptically before leaving.

The group looked at one another in shocked disbelief.

'It's like we've descended into hell,' whispered Elizabeth.

Ashling buried her head in Cara's neck and wished she could protect the child from all of this.

Later, lying sleeplessly in her bunk, Ashling watched Lou toss about in a fitful doze. She marvelled at his courage. Imagine trying to burst in on the Governors like that. They must have known they'd be punished, yet they did it for everyone's sake.

Lou was muttering in his sleep. Suddenly he cried out and sat upright. Elizabeth, who obviously wasn't sleeping either, quickly crossed over to him.

'It's OK, Lou,' she said soothingly. 'You're here with us. You're safe now.'

Jack joined them and also offered comforting words.

'You're quite the hero,' he said. 'You took on ...'

But Lou, his eyes wide and staring, clutched at Jack's arm.

'No!' he cried. 'Don't call me that. Don't call me a hero.'

'Why, Lou,' Elizabeth patted his sweating forehead. 'You're burning up. Try to get some rest, dear.'

Lou was shaking his head.

'It was my fault,' he said. 'It was all my fault. Ian ...'

'Of course it wasn't your fault,' began Jack. 'You did your best ...'

'No!' cried Lou again, shaking off Elizabeth's calming hand. 'I did it. I attacked them. It's my fault that Ian died.'

'Ssshhh,' whispered Elizabeth. 'Don't say things like that.'

But Jack touched her arm, looking all the while at Lou.

'Let him speak,' he said. 'I think he needs to speak, do

you, Lou?'

Lou nodded miserably. Ashling leaned forward in her bunk to catch his words. Could things get any worse than this? With Ian dead, what would become of the rest of them?

'We were being brought back from some lab where they did tests on our heads,' Lou was calmer now. Elizabeth held his hand and looked at him with concern. 'While we were passing along a corridor, a door was open and we could see two of those Governors inside. I was angry. I hated these people for what they were doing to us - I ran in and ... and I started to thump one of them.' He paused and wiped his forehead with his sleeve. 'The guards then began to mess me about. I was shouting. Ian dashed over and tried to come between me and them. He stuck into those Cobians, shouting at them to leave me alone. But they wouldn't listen. They hauled the two of us down to this ... this chamber where those cylinders are. Those cylinders Toby told you about. They didn't even give us a chance to explain; just shoved us into them.' He paused again. 'They shut down the visor on Ian's cylinder. It was made of perspex, so you could see his face ...' he made a choking sound as he remembered.

'I saw his face as he was being pushed into the chute.' He looked at Elizabeth. 'I saw his face, Elizabeth. I'll never forget his face. God!'

Elizabeth put her arms around him. She said nothing, but looked at Jack. There was nothing either of them could say.

Ashling drew back and buried her face in her pillow. Lou! It was Lou's fault that big, gangling Ian, who used to talk to her about playing guitar, was dead. He died trying to save Lou Gaffney. 'Brave, popular Lou Gaffney' had acted with his usual macho lack of thought and had caused Ian's death. She covered her ears to shut out the hushed whispering that was coming from the direction of Lou's bunk. She didn't want to hear any more.

Nine

As if in answer to Ashling's fears, several Cobians arrived after the sleep time and singled out herself, Cara and Dave.

'Hold on there,' shouted Jack as the trio were escorted to the door.'

'Where are you taking these people?'

'You can't just sweep them away like that,' broke in Elizabeth. 'They're youngsters, leave them be ...' But the pleas were ignored and the door closed, separating the group.

'Lay off, goons,' snarled Dave, trying to shrug off his guard. He was cut short by a blow on the head.

'There's no need for that!' exclaimed Ashling. 'You don't have to be so violent.' She was answered by a hateful glare from the Cobian. She could see the terror in Cara's face and felt angry and frustrated.

They were ushered into a lift which travelled very far downwards to a large laboratory. In the eerie semi-darkness, they were securely fastened into recliners, similar to the one Ashling had been in for her skin test. Then they were left alone. Ashling closed her eyes, as if to shut out the black fear.

'Why have they left us here, do you think?' asked Cara, her voice quivering.

Some ugly Cobian was probably scrubbing up before coming to ... she tried not to think ahead. She tried not to think that these might be her last moments alive.

'They're probably going to give us a haircut,' she joked. But even Cara wasn't fooled by her attempt at indifference.

She bit her lip and shut her eyes tight.

'What the hell is that?' Dave's voice made Ashling look up. She strained to see what he was looking at. In a gloomy corner was what appeared to be a huge tank. Slimy water reflected the faint light which emanated from a flickering monitor screen.

'Bloody hell!' exclaimed Dave.

'What? What is it you're looking at?' Ashling blinked to see better. As her eyes became accustomed to the gloom, she saw two shapes looming through the water. Her heart leapt as she made out eyes that were watching herself and Cara and Dave with still interest.

'What are they?' she whispered.

'They're like ... they're like seals,' said Cara.

'But bigger,' added Dave. 'A damn sight bigger.'

As the shapes moved closer to the side of the tank, their features became clearer; they were indeed shaped like seals, but there the resemblance ended. Spiny ridges ran along their backs. Small, humanoid arms protruded from beneath large, flabby gills on their chests. When they opened their mouths, as they did frequently, sharp teeth curved downwards into fleshy jowls. But it was the eyes that terrified Ashling; eyes that showed an intellect which was otherwise hidden in the mass of heaving grey flesh.

'Oh, my God!' she breathed.

'Are they,' Cara gulped. 'Are they going to feed us to those things, do you think?'

'No,' said Dave. 'Take a look over there,' he nodded towards the wall on his side. Ashling craned her neck to see, but it was out of her line of vision.

'What is it?' she asked. 'Tell me.'

'It's pictures,' said Cara. 'Like the ones I was telling you about. There are pictures of those ... things, those seal things and pictures of, I think it's us.'

'Go on,' said her sister.

'Well, there are coloured squares ... I can't make out ...'

'Coloured squares on the monsters and the same coloured squares on parts of us,' Dave cut in.

Ashling clenched her fists to keep from crying out. Transplants. The Cobians were surely going to take vital organs and transplant them into those seal creatures! She struggled against the straps. She shut her eyes; every part of her was tight with tension. She jumped as she felt hands at her straps.

'Dave!' she exclaimed.

'Shut up,' hissed Dave. 'For all their technology, their buckles don't stand up to what I learnt in the nick.'

Ashling rubbed her ankles as Dave was releasing Cara. She looked warily across at the tank where the monstrous creatures were showing signs of agitation.

'Come on,' said Dave, heading towards the door. He felt frantically along its surface for a button or lever, but the smooth steel revealed nothing.

'Damn,' said Dave. 'It's all bloody electronic.'

'Does that mean we can't get out, Dave?' Cara grabbed the lad's arm.

Dave was scrabbling furiously at the sides of the door in a desperate attempt at finding a release mechanism. 'Damn!' he said again as the effort proved fruitless.

The creatures in the tank were beating at the sides with their bony hands. One of them rose to the surface and emitted a piercing shriek that echoed around the room. Ashling put her hands over her ears against the awful, chilling sound. In a frenzy of frustration, Dave began to smash monitor screens and lab equipment.

'Stop, Dave!' Ashling shouted above the din. 'You'll only make things worse.' But Dave continued to furiously break everything in sight.

'That'll slow them up,' he panted.

The slimy water was splashing in green, viscous blobs on to the floor as the creatures battled against the sides of the tank. With a splintering crash the tank burst open and the creatures floundered on the wet floor, shrieking all the while. Ashling pressed herself and Cara against the wall as the grey shapes dragged themselves, with their puny arms, in their direction.

'Get back, scumbags!' Dave shouted at the massive hulks, pushing Ashling and Cara ahead of him towards the back of the lab.

Ashling looked back. What she saw made her stop; one of the creatures had a hand out, as if pleading. But, as well as that gesture, there were what appeared to be tears in his eyes.

'Wait,' she said, pushing Dave aside. 'I don't think they mean us any harm.'

'With those teeth? Don't bet on it,' retorted Dave.

'No, look,' Ashling stood still and gave a sigh of relief when the creatures stopped also. Dave and Cara seemed unsure of what to do, then they came and stood by Ashling. The creature held out its hand again and Ashling stepped forward.

'Don't, Ash,' whispered Cara.

'Things can't get much worse, can they?' said Ashling. She gingerly reached out and took the outstretched hand. She was surprised at how warm it felt. She looked into the creature's eyes and realised that it was trying desperately to communicate with her. 'It's OK' she whispered soothingly to the ugly thing, her own fears forgotten for the moment. With her other hand she patted its flabby face and was rewarded by a nod of acceptance.

'Come over, you two,' she said, without taking her eyes off the creature. 'They're not vicious. I was right.'

Dave and Cara approached and Cara touched the heaving side of the other creature. Dave watched, but made no move to communicate.

'Ugly buggers,' he said, but in a friendly tone. 'If you say they're OK,' he turned to Ashling, 'then that's all right by me.'

The calm moment was shattered as the door slid open and a group of armed Cobians burst in. The two creatures howled piteously as heavy blows fell on their clumsy bodies. As one, Ashling Dave and Cara thrust themselves between the helpless creatures and the Cobians.

'Go to hell, you miserable prats,' growled Dave. Cara

kicked out at the nearest Cobian, causing him to recoil with a hiss. The action caused the Cobians to turn their attention to the three humans.

Ashling tried to fight off the seizing hands. Dave fought viciously when he discovered that blows to their soft, scaly tissue caused more pain to the Cobians than it would to a human. He positioned himself in front of Ashling, Cara and the creatures and fought tirelessly. 'Leave them alone!' he shouted, sending one of the Cobians crashing to the floor. Ashling bit her lip as she waited for a response to Dave's action.

One of the Governors appeared at the entrance. He was dressed in medical garb, as if about to perform an operation. With dismay Ashling realised that he had probably come to perform the transplants. She caught her breath with the realisation that this man was to be the death of herself, her sister and Dave. A truly grim reaper.

The Governor watched, expressionless, for a moment before raising his hand for the fighting to stop. Then he looked with great deliberation around the wrecked lab and his eyes came to rest on Dave, with his bloody nose and torn clothes.

'Call off your stupid lizards,' Dave shouted, but they had already stopped.

'Why are you doing this?' asked the Governor.

'Doing what?' Dave was wiping his nose on a piece of torn clothing.

The Governor gestured to the cowering seal creatures.

'Defending these brutes,' he said.

'They're not brutes,' retorted Ashling. 'They're just helpless creatures and your lot were trying to kill them.'

One of the Cobians began to protest in his own language and the others joined in. The Governor held up his hand for silence again without taking his eyes off Dave.

'She's right,' Dave muttered. 'They were trying to kill those fellas there. That's what it looked like anyway.'

'Not kill,' the Governor said. 'Overpower.'

'Whatever it was, they were being bloody cruel about it,'

put in Ashling.

Suddenly she felt too angry to be frightened and a surge of power seemed to sweep through her body. She was no longer a timid little girl; between Jack's insistence that she be treated as an adult, and now defending these creatures, she realised that she was an important part of the group. They were all in this together and she must make her stand, however little she had to offer, and for whatever little time was left. 'There's no need for such force. They're harmless and gentle. Anyway it's probably your stupid genetic stuff that has made them the way they are.'

The Governor stared at her silently for a few moments. At first she felt shaken, both from her outburst and from the cold gaze, but all she had left was her anger and she returned his stare with a fierce glitter in her eyes.

She waited for the Governor to order that the three youngsters be strapped to the recliners again. She was sure that he'd want to eliminate them as quickly as possible now that they were making trouble. She gritted her teeth and edged closer to Cara. She would go down fighting bitterly and protecting her young sister.

Cara, encouraged by Ashling's outburst, clutched her hand and looked up at the Governor.

'Yeah,' she said, with all the anger of a small girl. 'You're rotten.'

With clenched fist and every nerve taut, Ashling poised herself to spring into action. However, the Governor said something to the Cobians who rounded up the seal creatures, along with Ashling, Cara and Dave, ushering them into a lift.

Dave began to resist, but intuition told Ashling that they'd had some sort of reprieve.

'Might be as well to go along, Dave,' she said, her anger almost spent.

Dave shrugged off a Cobian who had put a restraining hand on his shoulder.

'I wouldn't trust these creeps ...' he began.

'It can't get any worse than ... than this,' said Ashling.

'They could be taking us to that place where they shove people into space,' said Cara. 'Like they did to Ian.'

Ashling shuddered. She hadn't thought of that. She was beginning to quake inwardly after the confrontation and wondered would she have any fight left in her if it came to that.

'Not at all, Cara,' she said, but she knew her words were flat.

The lift eased to a halt and the doors slid open. They seemed to be in some sort of a terminus with several shuttles on rails standing idle. Very quickly the youngsters, along with the seal creatures, were pushed into one of these. Ashling's heart sank when she realised that none of the Cobians had entered the shuttle with them. As the doors slid to, she tried to hold down the panic she felt. Was Cara right? Were they about to be cast off into space? She glanced at Dave. His face was white and he was looking out into the blackness beyond.

With a smooth whirr the shuttle set off, out of the complex and across by the food processing place.

'Where do you think we're going?' asked Cara, her voice shrill with fear.

'Sit here, by me,' said Dave, patting the small space beside him and putting his arm protectively around the small girl. 'Whatever happens we're in this together.' Ashling looked at him gratefully. She felt she simply couldn't cope if Cara started to panic now. She must stay calm. She took a deep breath of the sticky air and sat the other side of Cara.

The seal creatures were making grunting noises. One of them leaned over and patted Cara's hand. He pointed out the window of the speeding shuttle and pointed to himself.

'What does he mean?' asked Cara. At first she was inclined to draw away from the creature, but the trust in its eyes prompted her to hold its hand.

'I don't know,' said Ashling.

'I think it means that we'll be all right,' said Dave. 'It doesn't seem upset, so it must know where we're going.'

He got up and looked around the small space, feeling the sides and poking at nuts and bolts. 'There are no controls,' he said. 'It must be run by remote.'

Now the shuttle was crossing the wasteland - a reddish-yellow, cracked surface that seemed to go on forever. The air got heavier and heavier and Ashling wondered was this their punishment for the fracas back there. Was death to be administered slowly in this metal tube, depriving its occupants of air in a slow, lingering, suffocating death?

After hours of gasping travel, a jagged line appeared at what seemed to be the end of the dome.

'What's that?' exclaimed Cara.

'It looks like ... like huts or something,' said Dave, squinting across the desert waste.

'Oh, lord!' said Ashling. 'What do you think will be there ..?'

Dave reached over and squeezed her hand.

'We're still together and we're still alive,' he said. 'And we've left the Cobians behind. Nothing could be worse than them.'

The shuttle drew to a halt at a shabby platform and the seal creatures indicated to the youngsters that they should get out.

'Come on,' said Dave. 'If we stay on this we might be ferried back to the Cobians.'

'Oh, I wish the others were here,' whispered Ashling.

'Me too,' said Dave. 'But they're not so we have to depend on ... on ourselves.'

The seal creatures led the way from the platform. Outside the platform area, Ashling, Cara and Dave were astonished at what they saw. For as far as the eye could see, there were lean-to shanties made from bits of metal and ragged fabric. They were arranged in no pattern - just a higgledy-piggledy mess. Shuffling between these hovels were shadowy figures with grotesque shapes.

Cara cried out and drew back, but one of the seal creatures took her hand again and patted it. It pointed to itself and then pointed towards the hovels.

'I think it wants us to follow,' said Ashling. She looked fearfully at Dave.

'Stick by me,' he said. Ashling knew that they would have little chance against any attack, but was impressed by Dave's courage. With feelings of almost disbelief they made their way through the maze of huts. Some of the populace shuffled over to gape at the newcomers, but the seal creatures grunted and acted as bodyguards. Other creatures stared at them with solemn indifference, their skeletal bodies huddled against the cooler air in this part of the planet. It was only now that Ashling realised that she could breathe more easily.

The seal creatures stopped near a muddy pool. With much heaving and grunting they began to move some sheets of metal towards a vacant space.

'I think they want to make a hut for us,' said Ashling.

The three of them nodded to show they understood and set about helping the seal creatures. There seemed to be endless heaps of metal and rags lying about.

'Where do you think all this stuff came from?' asked Cara as she threw some cloth over the teepee style hut.

'Probably from the time that the planet was ... was normal,' said Dave.

Ashling watched Dave working and talking reassuringly to Cara. She marvelled at how he had been transformed from a sullen ex-con, to a brave survivor.

When the hut was complete, they went inside. It was extremely primitive, but it sheltered them from the strange, dry wind that had suddenly risen.

It also gave them a sense of security. They regarded warily the shuffling creatures outside.

'They're just rejects,' said Ashling to Cara. 'They have no reason to attack us. We're just,' she swallowed, 'we're only rejects too.'

'And glad of it,' grinned Dave. 'I'd sooner be a reject here than be with that lot back there.'

His words reminded Ashling of their friends and she bit her lip. What would become of their friends?

Ten

Jack Brophy's attention was on the Governor standing at the door, talking to Toby. The Governor was looking intently at the group of anxious earth people, he was obviously discussing them. It was very unnerving.

'The children have been moved,' Toby eventually turned towards the anxious faces. Several hours had passed now and there was no sign of Ashling, Cara and Dave. 'They are safe and well and will come to no harm.'

'How do we know that?' asked Elizabeth, trying not to sound hostile. 'How do we know that they haven't been ... haven't been used?'

The Governor gave her a grim look and made to move away. Jack stepped towards him, his hand out. 'We must speak to you,' he said. 'Please, you must listen to ...'

The Governor looked at him coldly and moved outside. The door was sliding shut.

'Toby,' shouted Jack. 'You must make him listen ...'

Toby nodded slightly just before the door clicked shut.

Jack shook his head and looked back at the others. He beat the air with frustration. 'What do we have to do to make them see reason?' he said. 'They've got to tell us what they've done to the children and Dave.'

'How can we get them to do that?' Dan asked. 'We have no power over these people. We're completely at their mercy.'

'Mercy!' scoffed Elizabeth. 'What mercy?'

The other three looked at one another helplessly.

'I just hope,' said Elizabeth, 'that whatever they do, it ... it will be quick.'

'What do you think they'd intended to do with the three of us?' Ashling asked Dave as they sat together in the ragged space. The seal creatures had returned to their muddy pool nearby - they obviously needed water. Even though they were close, Ashling felt slightly threatened by the curious stares of passing mutants. Like the seal creatures, their eyes seemed to be the only evidence of any intelligence. Their bodies varied from twisted, skeletal frames to fat, wobbly creatures with mottled skin and tufted hair. Then there were others who, apart from slightly slanted eyes, resembled very slim humans. These latter had children who followed them about. All of them wore tattered clothing of soft material.

It suddenly dawned on Ashling how there was little evidence of children back at the complex - except for the few Cara said she'd seen.

'Those charts you talked about that were on one wall,' Ashling continued. 'Do you think they were going to ... to use us for transplants?'

Dave pursed his lips. 'I don't know,' he said. 'If they were, then what made them change their minds and put us down here?'

Ashling looked at him and smiled slightly. 'I think it might have something to do with the fact that you trashed their equipment, or had you forgotten?'

Dave grinned. 'Maybe being a trouble-maker has some advantages,' he said.

Ashling was surprised at how pleasant he looked without his scowl. His dark eyes crinkled and his pinched face took on a glow which seemed out of character with this dreadful place.

'I'm glad you're here with us,' said Ashling.

Dave turned towards her. 'Yeah?'

Ashling nodded.

Cara had fallen asleep on a pile of rags beside them. Suddenly Ashling felt an overwhelming desire for sleep too, but she knew that, if she lay down, any sleep would be invaded by nightmares.

They both jumped as one of the seal creatures re-appeared. He took Dave's hand and pulled him gently towards the door. Dave pulled back, but their new friend was insistent.

'I think he wants us to follow him,' said Ashling.

Dave pointed towards the maze of ragged 'streets' and raised his eyebrows. The creature nodded and pointed again.

'Suppose we might as well see what it wants,' said Dave.

Ashling looked doubtfully at the sleeping Cara and then at the ugly mutants that were shuffling by. She shook her head.

'You go, Dave. I can't leave Cara here.' Dave hesitated, but the seal creature pulled urgently at his arm again. 'Go on,' said Ashling, looking into the eyes of the creature. 'I don't think they'll do us any harm. In fact I think they're intelligent. You might learn something from him.'

'Are you sure ..?' began Dave.

Ashling nodded. She knew that Dave had reached a stage where he wasn't content to sit around. The recent fight, and now this change of place, seemed to have given him an extra shot of energy and confidence, made him realise that they must take survival into their own hands, now that they'd been separated from the others. 'We have to trust them. Apart from Toby they're the nearest we've come to having friends in this place. They're not going to harm us ... nor let us come to harm. Go on.'

She watched him disappear among the shambling bodies and rags and marvelled at her own courage. Up to now any thoughts of being left alone here would have filled her with unspeakable terror. Yet here she was, feeling sorry for them. What a far cry all this was from the night she was teasing Cara back in the kitchen. She pressed her eyes shut and wished she could wake up to find that all this was just a nightmare, that the stupid door was still banging and that none of this was happening. She shook the thoughts of home from her mind.

She was surprised when the second seal creature slithered in beside her. And pleased; no matter how brave she felt, it was nice to have some familiar form beside her.

'Hello,' she said.

The seal creature made a croaking noise and nodded its great head.

'I suppose that's your way of saying hello,' smiled Ashling. The creature touched her hand in a friendly gesture. Then it slithered across to where some metal tubing was scattered outside one of the ragged enclosures.

'What are you at?' asked Ashling. The creature settled beside her and threw back some rags to reveal a sandy floor. It smoothed out the sand with one hand and began to draw. Ashling watched with fascination as a shape emerged on the smooth sand.

'It's a figure,' she said. 'A human figure?' she pointed to herself. The seal creature shook its head and pointed across the waste land.

'A Cobian?' asked Ashling, as she pointed in the same direction. The seal creature nodded. Now it was drawing something else. It was a seal. Ashling pointed to the creature and it shook its head again.

'Like you? Something like you? And that's a Cobian,' said Ashling, pointing to the first figure. She knew it couldn't understand her, but she felt that it might at least understand her tone of voice.

Now it was drawing arrows from the seal to the figure. Ashling shook her head. The seal creature pointed to his own heart area and to Ashling's and became agitated in his desire to be understood. He jabbed again.

'Transplants!' exclaimed Ashling. 'There were transplants from one to the other.' She nodded to show she knew what he meant.

The seal creature smoothed out the sand again and made a fresh drawing. This time it was a large drawing of a creature like himself with arms and spines.

'Now that's you,' said Ashling, pointing to him. The seal creature nodded.

Then he began to draw a figure inside the image in the sand.

Ashling gasped. It was a Cobian.

'What do you mean?' she asked. She touched the drawing of the Cobian and touched the body of the seal creature. 'Is there a Cobian inside you?' She felt she was going to throw up.

The seal creature patted its head, then pointed to the head on the drawing.

'The head? Ashling wished she could understand. Then realisation hit her.

'The mind! You still have the mind of a Cobian!'

Through a series of drawings and much grunting, the seal creature revealed to Ashling how genetic engineering had first come about in an effort to create beings that could tolerate the changes in the planet. Most of these experiments had gone horribly wrong, resulting in the mutants that were wandering about this awful place. With her own drawings and symbols, Ashling wondered why these mutants were kept alive. The seal creature indicated that mostly they were left alone, but that sometimes they were used for further experiments because no more of the Cobians could be spared for such purposes.

'That's what they were going to do with us before ...' Ashling drew a picture of Dave wrecking the lab.

The seal creature nodded. Then he made some more drawings. These revealed that the mutants, though very bright, had lost all interest in living. They knew that they were condemned to remain here, either to waste away or else be used in more frightful experiments. They showed no interest in one another and rarely communicated.

He looked up hopefully at Ashling. Slowly she reasoned out his pleading look. He wanted help!

'Help?' she gestured hopelessly. 'How can we help?' The seal creature seemed to understand her and nodded enthusiastically. It pointed to her and to Cara and out to wherever Dave had gone. Ashling wished more than ever that the others were here. Jack and Elizabeth would know how to handle this. As it was, she simply shook her head. She was suddenly very tired and her head ached from concentrating and trying to decipher the seal creature's drawings. Through half-closed eyes, she watched the seal creature slither away towards its pool. If only she could help. If only she could do something. She wished Dave would come back.

She fell into a deep sleep and didn't hear Dave when he returned. He sat for a while, deep in thought about the horrendous genetic failures who shuffled about with hopelessness in their eyes, their bodies drooping with surrender to their lot. Then he too fell into an exhausted sleep beside the two girls. None of them were aware of the stirrings outside among the shadowy creatures of this place that the Cobians called The Pit.

Eleven

Back at the complex, the others were in a state of agitation when Toby and several guards came to take them to their work stations. None of them had slept and an air of gloom had settled over all of them.

'Toby!' Elizabeth ran to him when the doors slid apart. 'The children. Where have you taken the children?'

But Toby looked at her coldly and didn't reply.

'Toby,' she said again, not quite believing that he was behaving like this. 'You must tell us where they are ...'

Toby stood apart to let the guards usher the group to the lift.

Jack and Dan now joined Elizabeth. Lou, his face white and tense, didn't seem to know what to do.

'Are they safe, Toby?' asked Jack. 'At least tell us if they're safe.'

Toby nodded, almost imperceptibly. Elizabeth sighed.

'Why are you doing this, Toby? Why are you shutting us out,' she went on. 'I thought you were our friend.'

Jack touched her arm. 'Leave it,' he said gently. 'We have no friends here.'

'Oh God,' Elizabeth felt all hope draining from her. 'What are we to do? I just feel like lying down to die. I don't think I can stand ...'

'You'll do no such thing, Elizabeth,' Jack raised his voice. 'We'll carry on as we have been. We know we're doing something useful - you with your medical knowledge, Dan and I with our farming advice.'

'And where does that leave me,' Lou put in, with a note

of bitterness. 'I'm just fodder for their bloody experiments.'

'No,' said Elizabeth. She took his arm and glared defiantly at Toby. 'He helps me. At least do that for us.'

Toby nodded again.

'Now, come on,' said Jack. 'There's nothing to be gained by staying here arguing with this lot. Let's go and continue what we were at. It's the only way to stay sane in this hell-hole. If we show we can help we might have some chance.' He looked at Toby to see if there was any response, but Toby remained silent.

'Damn you, Toby,' spat Dan as he passed the Cobian. A flicker of reaction crossed Toby's face, but it was only for a second.

When the lift drew to a stop, they were parted, but Elizabeth kept a hold on Lou.

'Whatever you do,' she whispered, 'don't freak out when you see the sick creatures we have to tend.'

'Why do you think Toby has turned against us?' asked Lou.

Elizabeth shrugged. 'We just have to remember that we're not dealing with ... with people like us,' she said. 'Who knows what way their minds work? We were lulled into a false sort of security by thinking Toby was on our side. Now, it's like Jack says; we must each do the best we can in our own corner and hope that this shower of fishbrains will come to accept that what we do is important.'

'Thanks, by the way,' said Lou.

'For what?'

'For insisting that I help you. I'd resigned myself to heading off for another session in the lab.'

'We've got to stick by one another - what's left of us,' said Elizabeth grimly. Then she remembered that Toby had barely indicated that the children and Dave were all right. That was the only consolation she had to cling to.

Ashling opened her eyes, aware that something had woken her. She gave a cry of terror when she looked towards the rough entrance to the hut and saw a group of mutants crowded around it. Dave jumped up and moved over to her.

'What do they want?' she whispered.

'They must have followed me back,' said Dave. 'They don't look threatening. Look, they're just standing there.'

'Make them go away,' said Cara, now awake too.

Just then there was a commotion and the mutants moved aside as one of the seal creatures shuffled his way between them.

'It's OK,' said Dave. 'It's Zig.'

'Zig?' Ashling looked at him, puzzled.

'Zig and Zag,' said Dave with a dry grin. 'After those two puppets on telly, you remember? The ones that started on Dempsey's Den and then went to some English channel.

Ashling snorted and smiled.

'Anyway,' continued Dave, 'it's better than calling them seal creatures. He knows his name. Hi, Zig.'

The seal creature nodded and grunted. He ushered the mutants away from the doorway and sat down on the sandy floor.

'Zig took me through the whole place,' said Dave. 'It's just a shambles of hovels. All the reject mutants are dumped here to fend for themselves ...'

'I know,' said Ashling. 'The other ... Zag told me - with a lot of drawings and patience. It's awful.'

Dave was shaking his head slightly.

'No?' Ashling raised her eyebrows.

'Well yes. It is an awful dump, but the people ...'

'The people?'

'The mutants. They're not stupid ...'

'That's right,' put in Ashling. 'The ... Zag explained all that. Their minds are OK ...'

'They are. Except that they feel hopeless.' Dave was getting quite animated now. His face was glowing, as if he had some plan. Ashling looked at him for some clue, afraid to ask in case the sudden seed of security might disappear.

'They don't communicate much,' he went on. 'But they're surviving.'

'How?' asked Cara. 'What are they living on - out here in this desert place? They're not ..? They're not cannon ... cannim ... you know, those people who eat other people?' Her eyes were wide at the thought.

'Cannibals,' said Dave. 'Absolutely not. They're growing crops and eating them straight, not like the treated muck the Cobians ...'

'How can they grow crops?' Ashling interrupted him. 'This land is as dry as a bone.'

Dave was shaking his head. His tone was excited. 'There's a big hole in the dome,' he said. 'There's air and wind coming through it. And, at certain times the sun shines through. And I think the rain must have re-activated an old well years ago because they have a fairly decent river running along the far side of this ... this shanty town.'

'I thought all the air outside the dome was supposed to be poisoned,' said Ashling.

'I know,' replied Dave. 'But I think that it must have got purer over the past few centuries, or whatever time they have here.'

'How do you know all this?' asked Ashling.

'Zig told me. He drew pictures and grunted and made signs. The rest I've worked out.'

'But why are you looking so pleased?' Ashling asked. 'I know we've been spared those experiments and that we're all right. But don't you think that could end any time? That they'll come back for us when they've sorted out their cruddy lab again?'

'Maybe,' said Dave. 'But I think that, with the help from our two friends here, we might be able to muster this lot into some sort of action.'

Ashling looked at him incredulously.

'Are you out of your tree?' she laughed. 'You mean form an army and attack the Cobians? Get real, Dave. Those poor creatures couldn't form a queue, never mind an army.'

Dave frowned. 'No. Hear me out,' he said. 'You're forgetting that all these mutants or whatever they're called, they were once Cobians. The experiments changed their bodies - after all it was their bodies they were trying to make survive. But their minds are as good as ever. And,' he leaned closer to press home his argument. 'Remember that, for all their weirdness, the Cobians' minds are streets ahead of ours ... of earth people.'

Ashling scratched her head. She was confused. Dave made it sound so logical and yet ...

'Well, if they're so smart why haven't they revolted themselves? What's to stop them mustering up a bit of force themselves and clobbering the Cobians?'

'I don't know,' Dave admitted.

'Brainwashing,' said Cara.

'What?' Dave and Ashling said together.

'Brainwashing,' repeated Cara. 'I once read all about that. You can make people believe anything if you brainwash them.'

'Huh,' said Ashling. 'Don't be daft ...'

'No, she could be right,' Dave put in. 'They could have been convinced that they are worthless just to keep them in a state of uselessness. Like Cara said, the mind can be convinced of anything.'

'I don't know,' began Ashling.

'Well, at least let's see if we can get through to them,' said Dave. 'What have we to lose?'

'I'm game,' said Cara with childish enthusiasm. 'Come on, Ashling. If we don't do something we'll end up like them.'

Ashling looked at the two eager faces and then glanced at Zig, who seemed to have understood their eagerness. It was a completely loopy idea, but what choice was there?

'OK' she agreed. 'We'll give it a shot. Where do we start?'

Twelve

'How can you possibly be expected to cure all those people?' Lou asked as he looked at the lines of beds in the infirmary. Each bed was inhabited by a frail, skeletal figure, barely recognisable as a Cobian. They were covered with thin fabric of the same material as the suits that the earth group were wearing. It was a joyless, grey place with no attempt at comfort other than the beds. 'There are dozens of them,' continued Lou. 'Surely they have their own doctors ..?'

'They have,' agreed Elizabeth. 'But they think that my methods might bring in some long-forgotten cure.'

'And have they? Your methods, I mean. Have they helped to cure anyone?'

'No,' Elizabeth shook her head. 'I haven't quite worked out their anatomy and stuff yet. But I will tell you one thing ...' she stopped at the bedside of one of the ailing Cobians. 'The only thing I've been able to give is a bit of TLC.'

'TLC?'

She smiled. 'Tender, loving care. Well, tender anyway, whatever about the loving. And that has worked a treat. There's nobody taking up their beds and walking, nor no Lazaruses rising from the dead, but you can actually see a response when you talk gently to them and touch them.'

'Yecchh,' said Lou. 'I know how I'd like to touch ...'

'Yes, well that would be a great help, wouldn't it? Get your act together and go among the beds. Talk to them, touch them, pat their bony shoulders. Do anything that we'd do for our own at home. Haven't you ever comforted a sick friend?'

She smiled when she saw Lou's perplexed look. 'Well, I suppose a big, athletic fellow like yourself wouldn't have sick friends, would you?'

'I suppose I could pretend that they're friends,' he said.

'That's the spirit,' laughed Elizabeth. 'Here's a warm towel. You can pat brows with it. Very comforting.'

'Same towel for everyone?'

Elizabeth shrugged. 'If it gives them a bit of relief, well, sod the hygiene.'

Lou grinned and set off among the lines of beds. He hated being around sick people - ordinary sick people. The one time he'd visited a hospital he had thrown up. But these - he gritted his teeth with determination. By cripes, if it meant helping his own survival, he'd be Florence Nightingale.

'Well, how are we today, old frogface?' he said as kindly as he could muster to the frail being in the first bed.

'This bloody soil is all worked out,' Dan said to Jack, kicking up some of the dusty clay. 'It's exhausted. They must have been growing crops on it for years. There's no nutrients, except for the artificial stuff they spray on it.'

'I know,' agreed Mr Brophy. 'And I'd imagine that will only last for another short while.'

'What happens then?' asked Dan. 'What will they do for food then?'

Jack looked at him. 'To put it bluntly, old son, they'll be up the creek, without a paddle.'

'Which means that we'll be up the creek too,' said Dan. 'No food for them, no food for us.'

'Who says we'll be around that long?' said Jack, grimly. 'We both know that we survive here only as long as we're useful. Remember, we're only here because their original plan went wrong. They're not expecting much from us, so ...'

'So?' prompted Dan.

'So they'll get whatever little expertise we can give. After that, we're expendable, I'm afraid. Not something I'd discuss in depth with the others. But I think it's important that you and I know how it is.'

'You're probably right,' Dan sighed. 'After that business with Ian, I think we all know that we're on borrowed time.'

'And then the two girls and Dave,' added Jack in a low voice. He shook his head. 'If only they'd tell us. If only Toby would break down whatever barrier he's put between us and him.'

'Toby, pah!' scoffed Dan. 'We lost that creep long ago.'

'I can't think why,' mused Jack. 'I've tried to work it out, but I just don't know.' Secretly he thought it might have something to do with Lou's attack on the Governors, but he kept that opinion to himself.

'In the meantime,' he continued, taking a breath of the heavy air. 'In the meantime let's get on with the job in hand. If we look useful at least it might seem we know more than we do. Might make them hold on to us for a bit longer.'

'And do we tell them that their land is on its last gasp as far as growing crops is concerned?' asked Dan.

Jack shook his head. 'Not when we can't offer them an alternative,' he said.

Later that night, during the sleep time, Elizabeth, Lou, Dan and Jack sat listlessly on their bunks. Nobody spoke for a long time, each lost in a world of quiet desperation.

'Talk,' said Jack at length. 'Someone say something before we all go mad. How was your day, Elizabeth? Elizabeth?' His tone changed to one of concern as he saw, with surprise, that Elizabeth was weeping softly.

He rushed over to her. 'What is it?' he asked, taking her hands in his. 'Don't crack up on us.'

She pushed him away defensively and blew her nose. 'Damn you for noticing,' she said, trying to be cheerful. 'I'm all right.'

'Don't let it get to you,' said Jack. He smiled at the irony of his own words. 'Not that there's much we can do, but keep the old chin above water. If we crack now, well ...'

'I'm not cracking up,' said Elizabeth. 'I know,' she looked around, 'we all know now that this experiment is not turning out as the Cobians intended. It's just that ...'

'Yes?' Jack sat on the bunk beside her and put his muscular arm around her shoulder. This time she did not push him away.

'It's just ... just looking at those empty bunks. Ian and the youngsters. I don't think I can take ...'

'Yes you can. You must. We can't go under.' He shook her gently.

Elizabeth wiped her eyes with the back of her hand and looked at Jack, his square jaw set with grim determination to survive.

'And the Cobians,' Elizabeth added quietly. 'Every day there are more and more sick Cobians being brought into the infirmary. Today I finally diagnosed what the cause of their illness is ...'

'Malnutrition,' Jack interrupted her. She looked at him in surprise.

'How do you know that?'

'The land,' Dan had joined them. 'The land is clapped out and is becoming incapable of any more growth. They've worked it to the last. Soon they won't be able to plant any more crops.'

'How come everyone isn't suffering from malnutrition then?' asked Lou from his bunk. 'How come there's food for us?'

'Because the cases being brought in are suffering from long term malnutrition,' said Elizabeth. 'Whatever they're eating is providing less and less nourishment. It will gradually hit everyone ... including ...'

'Including us?' asked Lou, jumping down and approaching the others.

Elizabeth nodded.

'So that we'll either die of malnutrition too, or else they'll dump us because they can't afford to feed us?'

'That's about it,' admitted Jack. He was relieved now that Elizabeth and Lou knew the situation, even though he'd wanted to protect them from the awful truth. He should have known that Elizabeth would work it out.

'Looks like curtains for us then,' said Lou. He felt strangely calm as he said it. He wondered if it was because he knew for definite now that they were all doomed to die, instead of just speculating on that fact. 'You really believe in telling it like it is, don't you?' he looked almost angrily at Jack.

'He has to,' put in Elizabeth. 'We have to know what we're up against, no matter how awful.'

'Yeah, sure,' Lou grunted and ambled back to his bunk. 'You have to give us the bad news, don't you?'

Dan's lip curled as he watched the retreating figure.

'Prat,' he muttered.

'He's just a scared kid,' said Elizabeth.

'Like I said,' said Jack quietly. 'We must be prepared for anything. Let's try and get some sleep. At least our dreams can't be worse than this living nightmare.' He gently pushed Elizabeth's hair from her forehead and gave her a reassuring smile. 'OK?'

She nodded and pulled the cover around her. But, as the others made their way to their bunks, the door slid open and Toby entered.

Thirteen

'What is all that green stuff?' asked Ashling.

'There are all kinds of different things growing there,' replied Dave. 'But look, those daft morons have no order about them. They just wander in at random, take a fistful and eat it.'

'Well it's keeping them alive,' said Ashling. She leaned to look closer. 'There's some sort of cabbage and spinach, I think. That over there looks like celery.' She turned to Dave in amazement. 'They're almost like what we have at home.'

Dave nodded. 'That's it,' he said. 'I think that hole in the dome is what's responsible for all this. Look, there's a glimmer of sunlight coming through. When I was here earlier with Zig there was a mist of rain.'

'It's like ... it's like a whole new world,' said Cara.

'Old world,' mused Ashling. 'Bit like our own.'

'That's it,' Dave said enthusiastically. 'It must be what their world was like long ago.'

They were standing, with Zig and Zag and a crowd of mutants who had followed them, at the edge of a vast forest of greenery. A river, sluggish by earthly standards was meandering through the tall greens. Through a huge, gaping hole in the dome they could feel the air cooler and less sticky.

'The atmosphere outside must have righted itself,' said Ashling.

'This is neat,' said Cara, taking an exaggerated breath. 'We can breathe real air.'

'What are you grinning about?' Dave smiled at Ashling.

'I'm just thinking,' she replied. 'Did we ever think we'd see the day when we'd get so excited about fresh air and common veggies?'

Dave nodded. 'Gives a whole new meaning to life, doesn't it?'

'Well, what do we do now?' Ashling looked at the curious group who were watching. 'We can't even talk to these ... these people.'

'We've got to get them into some sort of order,' said Dave. 'If they had a bit of order and could communicate with one another, they'd make a pretty OK community.'

'How do we do that?' asked Cara.

Dave turned to where Zig and Zag were standing expectantly by.

'With their help,' said Dave nodded towards the two seal creatures. 'I'll tell you something I learnt in the nick and that is that proper nourishment and an ordered life are basics for survival.'

'What do you mean?' Ashling looked puzzled.

'Well, instead of them wandering in and just taking leaves according as they feel the need, they should have regular eating times. Get them to have organised eating times - as a community.'

'Like monks?' said Cara.

'Yeah, something like that,' said Dave. 'Monks, soldiers, convicts, workers ... families.'

'I get it,' put in Ashling. 'Eating together is a social thing. If we got them eating together then the next step would be to ... to get them into some sort of a team together.'

Dave was nodding enthusiastically. Ashling marvelled at his animated face.

Was this the sullen dork who hit out at everything and everyone such a short time ago?

He was twisting his hands nervously. 'What do you think?' he looked at her as if seeking approval. 'Is it daft?'

'Oh Dave,' she said. 'It's brilliant. It could work. We'll make it work.'

He glowed. 'You really think so?'

In answer, Ashling grabbed his hand. 'Come on,' she said. 'Before the idea gets cold. Let's try to explain to Zig and Zag just what we want. You do that, you're good with them. Cara, you scout around and see if you can come up with anything in that pile of scrap that we could use as dishes. Give them a wash in the river. I'll gather up a load of greens and break them into bite-sized pieces. If we serve them on dishes it will ... well, it will be as near as we can get to a proper meal.' She watched as her sister and Dave set off with the two lumbering seal creatures. This is happy, she thought. Happy in a different perspective, but still happy. She smiled and made her way towards the towering greenery.

Her chore took her deeper and deeper into the jungle of leaves. She was working so hard, making large bundles of food for the meal, that it was some time before she became aware of the eyes watching her. At first she smiled, thinking that the mutants were merely curious. But then they began to close in on her and to hamper her progress. She tried to ease past one tall mutant. His eyes glittered and he spat at her. That started the others hissing and they pressed forward menacingly.

Ashling backed away and realised with horror that there were more hissing creatures behind her. Some were brandishing metal rods.

Was this it? After all their enthusiastic plans, were herself and Cara and Dave simply going to be killed by these abandoned creatures?

'Go away!' she cried out in desperation. 'We're only trying to help you.'

But she knew she was wasting her breath. They couldn't understand. She was so frustrated that she felt like lying down on the ground. Let them kill me, she thought. At this stage there was nothing left - no hope, no reason to go on. Let them kill her and get it over with.

Then the image of Dave's enthusiastic face flashed into her mind. Dave, whose life had been one mess after another, one institution after another, who had been transformed into a brave and capable survivor. Dave who wanted to save these people from their miserable existence. They had no right to treat them like this.

She threw down the bundle of greens and stood defiantly against the crowd who were now very close to her.

'You stupid prats,' she shouted. 'Get out of my face. Back off! Go on.'

At first the nearest mutants recoiled slightly from her angry shouts, but then they pressed forward again.

'I said back off,' she shouted again. One of the mutants put out a hand and pushed her. Ashling was too angry now to be scared. 'Take your slimy hands off me, you creep,' and she pushed him back. Now several hands were grabbing at her. She was amazed at their strength. She thought up every dirty trick she could remember as she struck out at the grabbing hands. She gasped as a metal rod struck her a heavy blow across the shoulders.

'Damn you!' she cried as another rod caught her on the arm. She looked at the hostile faces and the raised hands and realised that she was about to go under the rain of blows. She felt a death-laden panic in her throat and put her hands over her head.

Suddenly there was a different commotion. She waited for the next blow, but gentler hands had a hold on her.

'Ashling! Are you all right?' she almost wept when she looked up and saw Dave. 'Thank God we were in time. Are you hurt?' He put his arms around her and she clung to him.

'I was sure I'd had it,' she whispered, looking over Dave's shoulder to where Zig and Zag were in animated communication with the mutants.

'They thought you were taking all that food for yourself,' said Dave. 'They're completely dependent on those greens for their survival. It's an unspoken agreement that everyone just eats enough to survive on. Anyone who disregards that gets killed.'

Ashling looked at the bundles she had so diligently

picked. 'No wonder they thought I was some greedy gut,' she winced as she laughed. Her lip had been split in the fray. 'Anyway, I gave them something to think about. They won't mess with me again. Silly prats.'

'You're a gutsy lady,' said Dave.

By now Cara had joined them. Her face was flushed from running.

'What happened?' she asked breathlessly. 'I heard shouting - you, Ashling. I heard you shouting.'

'I'm OK' said Ashling. 'These creeps got a bit excited, but I sorted them out. Anyway, enough about this. Did you find some things to use as dishes?'

Cara nodded, looking warily at the mutants who were still standing around.

'I got a whole pile of square bits of tin or something. I washed them in the river and they're stacked back there,' she pointed the way she'd come.

Zig and Zag made their way over to the three youngsters. Zig nodded and gestured with his hands. Dave nodded.

'OK Let's gather up this stuff and take it back,' he said. 'Zig and Zag are going to help too.'

'How do you know what he means?' asked Cara with wonder.

Dave smiled and looked at Ashling. 'Well, kid,' he said to Cara. 'I spent most of my days on earth grunting at people. I'm an expert in the grunt language.'

'Too right,' laughed Ashling. She was shaking from the fight, but was determined not to show it. 'And all that time you didn't know you were speaking Alienese.'

Feeling secure with Zig and Zag to help, the three youngsters set to, breaking up the greens and putting them on the square 'dishes' that Cara had found.

'Cara, is that all you got?' asked Ashling when the last dish had been filled. 'That's only about twenty. We'd need much more than that.'

Cara scowled. 'I can't work flamin' miracles. That's all there was.'

'It's OK We'll start with that lot,' said Dave. He took a rod and went over to Zig to explain, by drawing in the sand, that he wanted the mutants to sit in a circle and eat the food that would be served up to them.

Zig nodded. Then he and Zag organised a group of about twelve mutants to sit in a semi-circle around where Ashling and Dave stood with the heaped dishes.

'Right,' said Dave. 'Let's feed them.'

Cara and Ashling took the dishes around while Dave continued to communicate with Zig and Zag.

The mutants took the dishes, smelled them and looked expectantly at the two seal creatures. Zig and Zag said something in their own language to the group, who then looked at one another.

'They're not eating,' said Ashling. 'Why don't they start eating?'

'Maybe they're waiting for us,' said Dave. 'Take a dish each and we'll sit with them.'

The three of them sat into the semi-circle, Ashling easing herself painfully as she was still smarting from the blows.

'This is like Indians,' laughed Cara.

'Same idea,' said Dave. 'People gathered together for a pow-wow.'

The mutants watched for a moment as the three youngsters ate. Then they put down their dishes and got up. Ashling watched in horror as they shuffled away, leaving the dishes of greens untouched.

'Where are they going?' she cried. She looked towards Zig and Zag and was horrified to see that they were moving away too.

'Wait!' she called. 'Please don't go.' But the mutants paid no heed. The three youngsters watched them disappear into the maze of hovels.

Dave snorted and got up. 'So much for that bright idea,' he scoffed. 'I should have known it wouldn't work.'

Ashling got to her feet and went over to him. 'Don't knock it, Dave. It was a brilliant idea ...'

'Oh yeah?' he pointed to the untouched dishes. 'Tell me

about it.'

'We'll try again,' said Ashling. 'You'll see, it will work.'

Dave was shaking his head. 'No point. They've just no interest. It was a stupid idea. Bloody stupid. All they want to do is shuffle around this place until they die. That's all that's in front of us too,' he added bitterly.

'Don't say that!' exclaimed Ashling. 'We're not going to give up.'

Dave let out a sharp breath and sank into silence.

'What will we do now?' asked Cara. 'Dave? What will we do now?'

Dave just looked into the distance, his expression back to its original scowl. Ashling watched him for a moment. She felt a great surge of sympathy and wished she could do something to ease his disappointment. But the scowl sparked off something else. She thumped him on the arm. His head swung around and he looked at her with dismay.

'What was that for?'

'Don't do this,' said Ashling, evenly.

'Don't do what?'

'Don't go back to being a miserable drip with a chip on your shoulder. You've come a long way since then ...'

'Yeah,' Dave pointed to the untouched dishes and the big pile of greens they'd prepared. 'A really long ...'

'Shut up and listen to me,' Ashling raised her voice. 'So, it didn't work. At least we tried. So now we have to look after ourselves. And we'll do that. I nearly died back there in that jungle, but I'll tell you something, I intend to survive this place in spite of Cobians or mutants or anything else. So cut the sorry for yourself bit and get real. Don't desert us now. We've only got the three of us left.'

She realised she was shaking again after this outburst. Dave and Cara were still looking at her in amazement. She set about gathering up the dishes to hide her agitation. Dave came over to her. He was nervously pulling at his fingers. She could see that he was having difficulty getting the words out, but she just went on with what she was doing.

'You're right, Ashling,' he said. 'I was being a prat. I should have known - those mutants have been living like this for God knows how long. I shouldn't blame them for not responding. We'll look after ourselves. We'll move away from this crowd and set ourselves up nearer to the ...'

'Hey look!' cried Cara. The two of them looked up. Coming towards them from the maze of huts were dozens of mutants, led by Zig and Zag.

'They're carrying ...' gasped Ashling.

'Dishes,' finished Dave. 'They're coming back with the whole colony and bringing their own dishes! It's worked! The crazy idea has worked!'

Ashling was so overcome with relief that she squeezed Cara until the child cried out. They watched, fascinated, as the silent mutants began to form semi-circles of eighteen or twenty. With their dishes held before them, they looked expectantly, first at Zig and Zag and then at the three youngsters.

'There must be about two hundred of them.' said Dave in awe.

'Well, what are we waiting for?' Ashling sprang into action. 'Let's start feeding them. You two serve, I'll gather more greens.'

As she began to pluck the celery-type vegetables, she tensed up as she felt a presence beside her. She looked up to see several mutants do what she was doing.

'They're helping!' she whispered to herself. 'My God, they're helping!'

When she returned, the whole colony of mutants were sitting quietly eating the food that Dave and Cara were dishing out. Some of them had risen and were copying them, doling out the chopped up greens. There was an air of civilisation about the scene.

'This is the first step,' said Dave excitedly. 'Once we have them eating together at a certain time every day, then we can organise them into working groups. With Zig and Zag here to translate, we'll turn this into a proper ...'

'Community?' prompted Ashling.

'Exactly. There's a light at the end of the tunnel, Ashling.'

'What tunnel?' asked Cara, looking around. After all this she felt she could expect anything.

'He means that there's hope for us,' laughed Ashling, forgetting her bruises and her split lip. 'Hope for all of us.' She wished she could include Elizabeth and the others in that hope, but she knew that they were far removed from this land of reject mutants. All she could hope for was that they were still alive.

Fourteen

Everybody froze as Toby stood at the door.

'Toby ...' began Elizabeth.

Toby put his finger to his mouth and slid along by the wall until he came to the loo.

'What the blazes is he at?' muttered Dan as Toby beckoned to them and then pointed to the ceiling. 'What does he want?'

'Wait,' said Jack. 'Keep your heads down and your voices low. I think he means that the place is under surveillance.'

'But what's he doing at the loo?' persisted Dan.

'My guess is that it's the only place that's not bugged,' suggested Elizabeth.

'Better see what he wants,' said Dan. 'No point in all of us going or the newts above will get suspicious. You go,' he nodded to Jack.

'Yes', agreed Elizabeth.

'See if he knows anything about the ... the others,' said Lou.

Jack got up and stretched himself to try and look as natural as possible. Then he ambled across to the waiting Toby. His heart skipped a beat when he saw the anxious expression on the Cobian's face.

'Time has run out,' whispered Toby. 'The Governors have decided that the earth experiment is not worth continuing. Your work here is no longer of value to them. They know that nothing will reverse the damage that's been done over such a long time and that your efforts only serve to show us that fact. Our people are dying because our crops are getting less nutritious. You ... you ...' he hesitated.

'I know, we're taking food that's needed,' Jack finished the sentence for him. 'So, what happens next?'

'It has been ordered that your bodies be used,' said Toby.

Jack sighed. 'I figured that,' he said resignedly. 'It was only a matter of time. When?'

'After this sleep time,' went on Toby. 'The labs have been prepared.'

'Well, thanks for telling me this, Toby. I wish I didn't have to tell the others ...'

'I've come to help you,' said Toby. 'It's only a faint chance, but we must move very quickly.'

Jack looked at him in surprise. 'You're going to help? I thought ... we thought that you'd turned your back on us.'

Toby was shaking his head. 'I knew something like this was about to happen,' he said. 'I had resolved to help you. But I had to pretend that I no longer had any interest in you in case the Governors felt I was too involved and would move me. Now, there's no time to lose. Tell the others to come over here very quietly.'

Jack went back and whispered urgently to the other three. In a swift move, they were at Toby's side.

'Don't waste time by asking questions,' he warned. 'Just do as I say and this might work. The armoury is well guarded so I was unable to get anything to fight with. We are unarmed against the heavy weapons of my people. Be warned; the odds are very much against us. If anyone would prefer to stay and die painlessly tomorrow ...'

'We're all willing,' said Jack. The other three nodded.

'We'll go down with a fight,' said Lou with determination.

Elizabeth took one last look around the chamber that had been their home for ... how long now? She glanced at the bunks of Ashling, Cara, Dave and, of course, Ian. Their emptiness was a sad reminder of the four of them. Now would not be a good time to ask Toby what had become of the youngsters. She took a deep breath as he slid open the door and beckoned them out.

The metallic corridors seemed to echo thunderously no matter how softly the group pattered. Elizabeth felt sure her heart could be heard pounding. As they passed in single file, the door to a small chamber opened and Lou, who was at the rear of the line, found himself face to face with a surprised Cobian. He had the good sense not to cry out, in case there were others inside. The Cobian lashed out at him, grabbing him by the neck. Lou gave a strangled gasp as he felt himself lose consciousness. The noise caused the others to turn. Elizabeth, who was nearest, beat at the Cobian's face with her fists, but he still kept his grip on Lou. By now Jack, Dan and Toby had reached them. It didn't take much to overpower the frail and bony Cobian, but not before he had emitted a shrill screech which echoed along the labyrinth of corridors. Toby threw the Cobian back inside the chamber he'd just left and fiddled with the electronic lock.

'That will hold him for a little while,' he said. 'But he's alarmed the others. Come on. Don't stop for anything.'

Just before they moved off, he held up his hand and listened, his head cocked. Then the others heard it - a low rumble of running feet.

Toby nodded towards the entrance to another, smaller corridor and the group fled into it.

This became a pattern. Toby would pause, listen and direct them deeper and deeper into narrow, metallic alleys. The rumbles behind grew louder.

'I hope he knows what he's doing,' gasped Dan, his pale face shiny with sweat in the dim light that glowed along the corridors.

At last they came to an arch that seemed to lead to a bigger area. Toby peered around and beckoned them to come on. They were now in a different part of the complex. A huge window looked out on to a compound where a fleet of shuttle cars were lined up. Toby indicated that that was where they were headed. Now they came to stairs leading downwards. Suddenly a cry rang out over their heads. Looking up two flights of stairs, they spotted two alien heads peering down at them. A cry rang out again.

'Quickly,' said Toby. 'Just follow me. If they take the lift, they'll cut us off at the door. They're chief guards. Their weapons are the deadliest.'

As they ran down the stairs, an ear-splitting siren tore the silence. Shouts came from different directions and sounds of more running feet. Dan jumped on to the metal handrail on the stairs and slid swiftly to the bottom.

'Dan, what are you doing?' shouted Elizabeth as she saw him dash across the floor, away from the door they were meant to go through. 'Come back ...'

But Dan ignored her.

'We musn't stop,' Toby hissed as the group hesitated. He ushered them across towards the big doors. As they ran over the wide space, laser-type beams took chunks out of the floor around them.

'Spread out,' shouted Jack. 'Scattered targets,' he explained brusquely.

At least we'll die fighting, thought Elizabeth as bits of the floor surface hit her. Toby got the door open and stood aside to urge the others through. Glancing back, Elizabeth caught sight of rows of armed Cobians rushing down the stairs.

'Damn you, Dan,' she almost sobbed. Where had he gone?

'Come on!' shouted Jack, grabbing her arm. They followed Toby as he ran across the compound towards the shuttles. There was a high fence surrounding the area where the shuttles were housed. Toby was frantically pulling at the lock.

'It won't open,' he said. 'It only opens from inside!'

Lou quickly assessed the height of the fence. 'Is it electrified?' he shouted.

Toby shook his head. Taking a powerful leap, Lou clutched at the top of the fence. Sparks flew all around him as Cobians on a balcony shot at him. Within seconds he was over and had unlocked the gates.

'Run!' urged Toby, his Cobian face animated with apprehension.

'Shouldn't we lock it?' cried Jack as the group ran through.

'No time,' Toby shouted back. 'Just get away.'

'What about Dan?' panted Elizabeth.

Jack looked perplexed for a moment. 'Nothing we can do ...'

'Quickly!' called Toby as he opened the fly-up doors of one of the smaller shuttles. 'Inside!'

The group practically threw themselves in, laser sparks flying all about them. As the shuttle gathered speed they heard a cry behind; 'Hey!' a familiar voice shouted. It was Dan galloping after the speeding shuttle, a troop of armed Cobians close behind him.

'It's Dan!' shouted Lou. 'Leave the doors open.'

Toby pressed a button and the fly-up doors opened again. Lou leaned out, his legs held by Jack. At least they're not shooting at us for the moment, thought Elizabeth when she saw the Cobians dashing towards the other shuttles.

'Let me go a little more,' shouted Lou. Jack reached up to give him a longer stretch. With a superhuman leap, Dan caught one of Lou's outstretched hands. His body was being pulled along the sandy surface.

'I can't hold him much longer!' cried Lou. 'He's slipping.'

Elizabeth climbed past the straining shoulders of Jack. Holding the open door, she reached out towards Dan. He looked up helplessly as he held on to Lou. He tried stretching his free hand, but couldn't reach Elizabeth.

'We're going to lose him,' shouted Lou, with a note of panic.

'Like hell we are!' Elizabeth shouted back. 'Hold on with all your might.'

She gripped Lou's track suit top and eased her way precariously along the ledge where the door met the chassis of the shuttle. With a determined sweep she grabbed Dan's sleeve. As she gained more purchase, she could feel his body begin to draw closer.

By now the pursuing shuttles were speeding this way. She tried to shut them out of her mind as she concentrated on easing Dan into the shuttle. Now sparks were exploding around them. It would only take one near hit to upset the balance and cause them to lose Dan.

'Oh, come on Dan,' she almost sobbed. Her nails were broken and her wrists felt like they were about to wrench away from her arms. With one mighty swoop, she caught Dan's collar and heaved. His feet were off the ground.

'Gotcha!' shouted Lou, grabbing Dan's back. 'Pull,' he called to Jack. They all fell back in a heap on the floor.

Toby immediately pressed the lock controls on the console in front of him and the doors swung shut.

'Hold on to each other,' Toby shouted as the engine roared into faster action. Looming ahead was the high wire fence on the other side of the compound. Toby knew he was taking a dreadful chance; always, just before sleep time, the electric current was programmed to come on. If that had been done, then they would all die. He checked the time gauge. There were only seconds left. He pressed the accelerator button to get the last ounce of speed. The digital time gauge turned relentlessly.

Three seconds to go. Gripping the steering bar tightly, Toby aimed the shuttle at the fence. Just before impact, he closed his eyes. There was a terrible jolt and all of them were thrown around the small shuttle. The time gauge slotted to nought and Toby glanced back to see the torn fence sizzle with blue sparks as the programmed electricity switched on.

The pursuing shuttles were lined up in confusion at the broken fence, none daring to cross the broken, blue-sparked electric fence.

'Well done,' said Jack, picking himself up and offering a hand to Elizabeth. Toby smiled. Little did they know just how close they'd come to death.

'Where did you get to?' Elizabeth turned to Dan who was nursing a bleeding hand. His clothes were in shreds and his legs were badly grazed. His face was white with dusty sand. 'We thought you were lost ...'

Dan grinned. 'I saw the lift doors,' he said. 'Toby said the chief guards had the deadliest weapons - though I don't see how they could be worse than those laser things ...'

'Much worse,' Toby said grimly. 'The chief guards' weapons are designed to horribly maim their victims - a sort of living death to punish wrongdoers. Believe me, you would prefer to die by laser.'

'Whew!' exclaimed Dan.

'Go on, anyway,' said Elizabeth impatiently.

'I spotted the electronic control panel on the ground floor and smashed it,' said Dan, with a dry grin.

'Jeez, Dan,' said Jack. 'If it hadn't worked ...'

'I know,' said Dan. 'But it did. And we're here.'

'Don't bet on it,' said Lou from the back. 'There's a fleet of shuttles coming through the other gates.'

Nobody spoke as they watched Toby urge the shuttle to go faster. Outside, clouds of dry, yellow dust flew up against the windows. The air inside the shuttle was getting hotter and the earth group's hair dripped sweat on to their faces.

'Hell!' exclaimed Dan.

They peered through the dusty windows and were aghast to see a line of shuttles draw level. Their own shuttle shook as a beam hit the side. Then another, and another. Toby kept his eyes firmly ahead.

'Move away from the windows!' he shouted.

No sooner had they done so, than a side window shattered as a beam struck it. Elizabeth watched with horror as the beam burnt a hole in the fabric lining the opposite side. If that was flesh, she thought and shivered.

The smouldering fumes filled the small compartment and everyone choked and coughed. Now another beam shot through and did the same damage. By now all of the windows were shattered and more and more burning holes were appearing.

'Use your feet,' yelled Jack above the awful noise.

'Stretch across your feet and try to stamp out the fires.'

He didn't need to say it again as the other three kicked at the flames, praying silently as they did so that no beam would hit a foot.

Suddenly things got quieter. No more beams were coming through the broken windows. Lou risked raising his head.

'They've stopped!' he cried. 'They're all lined up back there - they seem to be turning.'

The others raised their heads also and shouted with relief at what they saw.

'Can you see, Toby?' said Lou. 'They're turning back.'

Toby nodded. He was slowing down the shuttle. As the dust cleared, the group were amazed to see a small platform ahead, beyond which was a long, high wall.

'What is this place?' asked Dan as they all peered out.

'This is The Pit,' said Toby. 'That's why our friends have turned back. The only way my people come here is in heavily armoured vehicles. No Cobians ever come this far in light shuttles. This is hostile territory.'

'And this is our ... our destination?' whispered Elizabeth.

Toby nodded. 'It's where the children were brought.'

'The children?' Elizabeth clutched the Cobian's hand. 'They're here? Are they safe?'

Toby shook his head miserably. 'I don't know,' he replied honestly. 'But I've brought you here in case ... in case they're still alive.'

'Have we stepped from the frying pan into the fire?' asked Dan bitterly, his bleeding hand tucked under his other arm.

Toby looked at him with a puzzled expression. 'What do you mean ..?'

'Never mind, Toby,' said Jack. 'You've saved us from the Cobians and we're eternally grateful. Now, let's see what this place has in store for us. Aren't you coming with us?' he asked as Toby hung back.

Toby shook his head. 'This place is inhabited by grotesque mutants,' he said. 'Experiments in genetic engineering carried out by my people. Experiments that went horribly wrong. The maimed creatures were taken out here ...'

'And dumped?' said Elizabeth. 'You mean they were just taken out according as each experiment went wrong and left to fend for themselves in this wasteland?'

Toby nodded. 'So you see why I cannot accompany you. These people, whatever survivors might be left, hate me and my people for doing that. Can't you understand that? And if I am with you, it will endanger you too.'

'But aren't they your people too, these mutants?' asked Elizabeth. 'Weren't those experiments carried out on your own people?'

'All the more reason for them to hate us,' said Toby.

'But what will happen to you when you go back?' asked Lou. 'They know you've helped us. You won't be flavour of the month back there either.'

'I'll be put on trial,' said Toby.

'And get roasted,' put in Elizabeth. She took Toby by the arm. 'Listen, sunshine,' she said firmly. 'You come with us. You're our friend and we're all in this together. Whatever is here, we'll face it together.'

The other three nodded in agreement.

'But they'll kill you if you're with me,' persisted Toby.

'We survived your lot, we'll survive this lot,' said Elizabeth. 'At least we'll make a jolly good attempt.'

Fifteen

'That's right, nearer the hole in the dome,' Ashling was saying. She was standing near the huge hole with a group of mutants. With her hands she was trying to explain to them that it was healthier to build their huts nearer to the fresher air which was coming in through it. Up to now the mutants had kept their distance from the hole. According to Zig they believed that, if they went too close to it, they would be sucked out into the atmosphere.

It had taken a lot of patience to explain to them that it was because of the hole they were all surviving so well. Now Ashling was getting them to move away from the sandy waste where they had their ragged shanties and become a more ordered colony in a healthier spot.

This is really paying off, she thought with a certain amount of pride as she watched the mutants setting up their huts in rows, leaving passages between, like primitive streets. She gazed reflectively at a rectangular sheet of metal lying on the ground. It reminded her of the shed door she had gone out to fasten on that fateful night. What a funny hand life deals out, she mused. Her preoccupation at that time had been discos, boys, the latest gear, and keeping Cara out of her hair. Totally self-oriented. Now look at me, she smiled, hands filthy and calloused from working with an ex-con to help in the survival of a whole community.

She felt a warm glow as she watched Dave confidently give instructions to the mutants. He caught her eye and laughed. People are what matter, thought Ashling. Not the labels that class structure imposed on them, but people themselves. At home Dave would have been totally out of her scene. But now, she waved back at him, here he was an affectionate part of her existence.

How ironic that she should grow into a clear-sighted maturity out here on this God-forsaken planet.

By now the three youngsters had convinced the mutants that they were on their side. After several hiccups and false starts, the mutants were beginning to work together to create better living conditions. Meals were taken, at the end of each working day, in a wide compound which Dave had created.

'How did they get like that in the first place, I wonder?' Ashling said to Dave as they were all working in the old settlement, tearing down the old huts to take through the jungle of greens to the new site.

'Like what?'

'Alone. Solitary. How come they didn't try to organise themselves?'

'I think it was Elizabeth who said that they were becoming so cold-blooded they just lost interest in one another.'

'And don't forget the brainwashing,' put in Cara.

Ashling smiled. 'Of course. You're the one who pointed out that they were brainwashed. But I still can't understand why they didn't react when they were dumped out here. At home people unite during the most awful wars and things. In fact they unite especially during terrible catastrophes. You'd imagine that these would have done the same. Even unite in their hatred of the people who put them here.'

'Who knows?' said Dave. 'Just remember that these are not people. They're not like us ...'

'Yes, but they were once. Toby told us that.'

'Well at least they're getting more like people,' piped up Cara. 'The huts near the hole are beginning to look like a sort of village. And the whatsits ...' she pointed to the creatures.

'Mutants.'

'Yes. They're starting to do things together. They do what you tell them, Dave.'

Dave blushed. 'Well, me and Zig. I couldn't do it without him.'

'Yes, but you're the brains behind it,' said Ashling. 'You have them grouped into working teams to make better huts and stuff.'

'And what about you?' said Dave, looking at Ashling. 'You have a very nifty team providing meals for everyone each evening. That's the first step in organising a crowd who don't speak your language. Only for that ...'

'That sounds very sexist,' laughed Ashling. 'The woman organising the meals while the men organise the huts.'

'Does that bother you?' asked Dave. 'Woman's place and all that feminism stuff.'

'At h ... in another place, yes. Definitely. But here? Not a bit of it,' laughed Ashling. 'I'm just so glad to be alive that I'm willing to do anything to make a go of this. It is working, this plan of ours. That's what matters. It feels nice to be exhausted from hard work every evening.'

'If Ma could hear you say that, she'd ... she'd ...' began Cara. She stopped and the three of them fell silent. Ashling squeezed her eyes shut and tried not to think of home. Dave put his hand on her shoulder.

'At least you have happy memories of home,' he said. 'Me, well I never had a proper home. My old man scarpered when I was eight.'

'And your mother?' prompted Ashling.

'Married a nutter who thumped me around. I left when I was twelve. Got in with a gang. We used to knock off shops and cars.' He looked at Ashling to see if she was shocked. She was.

'Did you get caught?' asked Cara.

'Yes. Shunted around from one institution to the next. Once you have a record, no one wants to know you. No one will give you a job. So you switch back to bad company, because they're the only ones who'll have you, and the whole thing starts over. I once got a job on a building site,' he went on. 'I really liked that. I used to dream that one day I'd have enough money saved to put myself through school and become an architect - design super buildings. Daft idea, that.'

'That's not daft,' said Ashling. 'If we don't dream we don't get what we want. What happened? Did you stay on in that job?'

Dave shook his head. 'Some bastard snitched that I had a record and the foreman gave me my walking papers.'

'What a rotten thing to do,' said Ashling.

'Yes, well that's all in the past,' said Dave. 'It's now that's important ...'

'What's wrong?' asked Cara, pointing to the mutants. They were becoming agitated and were rising. An excited chattering broke out and they began running back towards the tall greens.

'Wait!' shouted Dave, getting up and running towards them. 'What is it? What's wrong?'

'Ssshhh, listen,' said Ashling, getting up too.

Dave and Cara stopped and listened. There was a rumble of engines coming from the desert outside the wall.

Ashling's heart sank.

'Cobians,' she whispered. 'Oh God. Just when things were ... I should have known it was too good to last.'

'Damn, damn,' Dave watched the frightened, retreating mutants. 'If only I'd had time to get this lot organised into a fighting band. Damn!'

'Will we hide?' asked Cara, trying to keep the panic out of her voice.

'What's the point?' said Dave. 'They'd find us. Better just stand our ground.'

The three of them stood together, facing the entrance through the wall, away across the sandy wasteland. Dave reached out and took Ashling's hand and squeezed it. His other hand he put on Cara's shoulder protectively.

Ashling gasped as two figures, then a third and a fourth came cautiously through the entrance.

'I don't believe it!' she said. 'It's Jack and Elizabeth ... and Dan and Lou!'

'And Toby,' added Cara. 'Isn't that Toby behind them?'

With a shout the three of them ran towards the newcomers. Across the cracked, sandy waste they fell on one another in joyful reunion.

Everyone began to speak at once.

'Thank God you're alive,' said Elizabeth, her arms around Cara. 'I honestly thought we'd never see you again.'

Jack whistled when he saw the remaining huts from the original settlement. They were now obviously idle and falling apart.

'So this is where they lived, the mutants.'

'Lived?' said Dave.

'Aren't you alone?' asked Jack. 'I don't see ...'

Dave laughed. 'We've moved them. We're all living beside the river now.'

'What?' Jack looked incredulous.

'Beyond those old hovels, across the sandy area, there's a hole in the dome,' explained Dave. 'Some rain and sunshine get through ...'

'And there's a jungle,' put in Cara.

Elizabeth looked at Ashling and raised her eyebrows. 'Is that true?' she asked.

Ashling nodded. 'There are vegetables and fruit growing.'

The group went excitedly past the old huts and stopped in amazement as the green jungle loomed.

'Good grief!' exclaimed Dan.

They made their way through the greenery and out the far side where the new 'streets' were. At the sound of non-hostile voices, the mutants began to appear from their huts.

'So, these are the rejects that you told us about, Toby,' whispered Elizabeth.

'They're mega ugly,' observed Lou.

'We don't notice that any more,' Ashling was feeling quite protective towards 'her' mutants. 'They just want to survive, like us.'

However, one of the mutants was pointing, jabbing his finger angrily towards the newcomers.

'It's all right,' Dave shouted. 'They're friends.' He put his hand to his heart in the gesture they'd been using to indicate friendship. 'Friends.'

But now more of the mutants were behaving in an agitated manner. Zig and Zag appeared from the river bed where they'd made their home. Dave tried to get them to explain to the mutants that these people were friends. But Zig and Zag were staring beyond the earth people at Toby. Zig made a hissing sound and it dawned on Dave that it was Toby they feared.

'I don't think they like us,' said Dan.

The mutants were now moving as a group towards Toby. They looked menacing.

'Wait!' shouted Ashling, putting herself between Toby and the mutants. The others followed her example. Dave pushed the advancing mutants back, indicating all the while that Toby was a friend. They stopped, as if unsure what to do next. Zig and Zag finally accepted Dave's signals and called off the threatened hostility.

'That was close,' whispered Elizabeth as they drew back. 'I've had enough excitement for one day.'

'It's all right,' said Ashling. 'They'll accept what Dave and Zig say to them. They're not going to harm anyone.'

'Come on,' said Dave. 'Let's show you what we've been at since we saw you last.'

The newcomers marvelled at the lush growth of greenery and the clear water in the river.

Jack lifted a handful of soil, pressing it between his fingers and sniffing it.

'That's rich, fertile soil,' he said. 'I'd say you could grow anything on this.' He offered it to Dan who rubbed it expertly between his palms.

'It's good,' he said. 'Very good.'

'Do you think you could do something with it?' asked Dave. 'The soil. Could you farm it properly? The mutants simply let things grow by themselves. I don't know anything about farming stuff, but I figured that there must be some way to use it better.'

'I have no doubt,' said Jack. 'We could plan a rotation of crops. It's a lot of work. It would take a long time for the few of us ...'

'Oh, we can get all the help we want,' said Dave.

'What?' Mr Brophy looked at him in surprise.

'The mutants,' explained Dave. 'We've got them to the stage that we've only to show them what we want done and they'll do it.'

'You've achieved all that?' exclaimed Jack.

Dave nodded. 'Well, we had help from those two seal creatures. But the mutants are very intelligent. Their bodies are maimed through those stupid experiments, but their minds are fine.'

'Their bodies look healthy,' said Elizabeth. 'I know they're misshapen, but I can see from the way they move that they're healthy beings.'

'And strong,' said Ashling, her eyes sparkling with happiness. She looked proudly at Dave. 'Dave has given them back their dignity.'

Dave grimaced good-humoredly. 'Posh words,' he muttered. 'You know well that it was the three of us who got things going.'

'Yes,' put in Cara, slightly miffed. 'I worked real hard ...'

Ashling laughed and messed her sister's hair.

Elizabeth looked at Jack who seemed to be lost in thought. She leaned over and put her hand on his. He put his other hand on top of hers. Ashling noticed with surprise the gentle look that passed between them. Jack and Elizabeth? Well, why not? Convent rules were in the distant past and besides, people need the comfort of each other at a time like this. She glanced at Lou - every girl's dream back at school. Popular, preening Lou. Poor Lou; he would always have to carry the burden of knowing he'd indirectly caused Ian's death. The god of 5A was really a pathetic little boy who responded to his fears by lashing out. She knew she would never stumble, stutter and blush in the presence of Lou Gaffney types ever again. She sighed when she remembered that there would be no more such boys in her life.

'What are you thinking?' Elizabeth was asking Jack.

'I'm thinking hope,' he said.

'Hope?'

'Yes. Those incredible kids have succeeded in doing so much with these ... these people in such a short time, think of what we can all do now that we're together again - plus the fact that we have Toby to translate for us. I think we just might save ourselves and this planet.'

Sixteen

'Look at them,' Elizabeth said to Ashling as they looked up from digging a channel through an area of land beside the river. With a team of mutants and under Dan's direction, further fertile areas were being created by irrigation.

'Who?' asked Ashling, straightening up and stretching.

'Jack and Toby. They're deep in serious discussion. I wonder what they're on about.'

'Probably something to do with the dome or stuff like that,' said Ashling.

It was generally agreed that the dome had become obsolete. Since there had been no pollution from the planet into the outer atmosphere for so long now, the air outside had purified again. If they could gradually pull down the dome, the whole planet would return to its original state. The problem was that the dome was so high and there was no way of getting at it. All they could do at the moment was to utilise the area around the hole to the very utmost.

'You like him, don't you?' Ashling resumed work with the primitive tool that the mutants had made.

'What?' Elizabeth looked at her.

Ashling smiled. 'Jack. Aren't you in love with him?' Cripes, was she really saying this - and to a nun? Elizabeth made funny noise and Ashling thought perhaps she'd gone too far. But when she looked up, Elizabeth was smiling.

'You don't miss much, do you? Yes, I've become very fond of him and he's pretty fond of me too. It happens - it's as old as mankind.'

'But what about ..?' Ashling nodded to the cross that

Elizabeth still wore.

'Being a nun, you mean?' Elizabeth said. 'Yes, I must admit it gave me some anxious moments. But I don't think the good Lord would expect me to be a one woman convent, especially under these circumstances. Things change. Different values become important, values that don't make one any less of a person. Can you understand that? Or are you shocked?'

'Shocked?' snorted Ashling. 'After so long in this place nothing would shock me any more. No, I'm delighted for you. Delighted for Jack too. I've always liked him. He's very clever and, since I was a small kid, I used to feel that when men like Jack and my father were around nothing bad could happen.' She laughed. 'Little did I think then that I'd be feeling like that up in space! I still feel sort of secure having Jack here, but I know too that bad things can happen and that I've got to face them myself.'

Elizabeth looked at her thoughtfully for a moment. 'You've grown up, Ashling,' she said.

'Yes,' agreed Ashling. 'I know.'

Later that night, as the earth group and Toby sat together in the hut they had built for themselves near to the hole in the dome, Jack nodded at Toby and began to speak.

'I'm afraid the time has come for action, folks,' he announced.

'What do you mean?' asked Dan.

'We have the basics for survival over here, in this small part of the planet,' went on Jack. 'But we need more.'

'What are you saying?' asked Elizabeth. 'Surely, with all the organising we're doing - all those work parties doing great things ...'

Toby was shaking his head.

'Jack's right,' he said. 'There are two important items we need. One is a laser beam which we need to take away the rest of the dome. These mutants have families. The increasing numbers would eventually prove too much for survival in this small area. We've got to let in more sunlight and pure air so that we can grow more crops.'

'And that leads to the second thing,' put in Jack. 'Toby says that there are huge containers of a type of wheat grain frozen back at the complex. We need to have grain - just having fruit and vegetables is not sufficient for our diet. We also need medical supplies and tools.'

'So we need to take control of the complex, is that what you're saying?' asked Elizabeth. 'How do we propose to do that?' she went on when Jack nodded.

'Attack?' suggested Lou.

'I'm afraid so,' said Jack.

'Oh no, not that,' groaned Elizabeth. 'Can't we just go on as we are. Those others, your people, Toby, they're frail and ... dying out. I've spent so much time with them in the infirmary. The Governors and those ... those guards, they're all going to die out anyway. Couldn't we just leave things as they are?'

'We can't, Elizabeth,' said Jack gently. 'We need what they've got if we're to really get this place living again.'

Elizabeth got up angrily. 'You men are all the same. No sooner do you settle in one place than you want to do battle. Leave me out of this.' She got up and went out into the slight breeze that was coming in through the hole in the dome.

Ashling felt that she ought to go and reason with her, but she wanted to hear the rest of the plan. She realised that Jack was right, but how did they expect to take on the armed Cobians? She drew up her knees and rested her head on them. How was it that, just when happiness was within one's grasp, something else turned up to dissolve it? She closed her eyes and suddenly felt very weary.

Seventeen

'And remember,' Jack was saying to the mutants through Toby. 'No matter what happens, keep these shields firmly around you. They are laser proof - Toby knows that. If we can simply get close enough for hand to hand combat, we have every chance of success; the Cobian flesh is soft and vulnerable and we'll easily overpower them.'

Toby's help in training the strongest mutants into a fighting force had been invaluable. Lou had used his knowledge of physical fitness to make them even stronger and fitter.

Using the metal which lay around in abundance, other teams had worked at making large shields which, when put together by the body of 'soldiers', would create a wall of protection against the laser guns. The time had now come for the assault. The whole colony assembled at the entrance to the desert wasteland which led to the Cobian complex. The long march was due to start.

'I still don't like this,' said Elizabeth as she held Jack's hands. 'I wish it could have been done some other way ...'

'What other way, Elizabeth?' he said. 'We've been through all this. Let's not make it more difficult.'

Ashling chewed her lip. She felt exactly as Elizabeth did, but she knew this assault had to go ahead. She hugged Dave. Over his shoulder she saw Lou watching. He turned his head away when he caught her looking. She knew his struggle to become a valuable part of the group - and he had succeeded. He too had had a lot of growing up to do. But she also knew that, in moments of stress, the old Lou could emerge. His attitude towards Dave remained superior and he sometimes showed resentment on seeing Ashling in Dave's company.

'Just ... come back,' Ashling turned back to Dave.

He grinned, picking up his shield and tying his water bottle to his belt.

'I'll be back,' he said. 'We'll all be back. You stay cool.'

There was a lot more Ashling wanted to say, but she knew that, if she tried, she would end up blubbering and she certainly didn't want that.

She simply nodded. She knew she didn't need to tell Dave that she wouldn't rest easy until he returned. He'd know that. She went over to Lou. He regarded her with slight suspicion for a second, but she smiled. This was no time for petty differences.

'Take care, Lou,' she said. 'We want you all back safe.'

'Thanks,' he muttered.

With Elizabeth and Cara and the remaining mutants, including Zig and Zag, she stood watching until the bizarre army had disappeared across the cracked, yellow desert.

'Do you think they'll be all right?' Ashling sought reassurance from Elizabeth.

Elizabeth sighed and shrugged. 'I don't know, Ash. I really don't know.'

'Here come the outer guards,' muttered Toby. 'There are only about thirty of them. They're the strongest. Remember, surprise is a great weapon. They're not prepared for anything like this. If we can get past them, we'll have a fairly reasonable chance ... Keep the shields together!' he shouted first in English and then in his own tongue as the first beams hit the metal.

The shields had been designed to slot together and the marching group did this. It was hot behind the metal, and getting hotter as the beams heated it. The earth people and the mutants clutched the primitive weapons which had been fashioned from scrap.

'Now!' shouted Toby. They had reached the guards.

With a cry, they unslotted the shields and set about the surprised Cobians with clubs. Their soft flesh was no match for the stronger, now healthier mutants and earth men. The guards retreated farther and farther back towards the complex. The inner guards, afraid to hit their own looked on helplessly at the advancing mutants who were holding the frightened outer guards as extra shields. Inside the complex there was a confusion of bodies as the Cobians, long out of practice in combat and ill-prepared for the surprise attack, fell into disarray.

As planned, Toby and Jack, along with a formidable foursome of well trained mutants, left the others and slipped along the labyrinth of corridors.

Jack gave one nervous glance backwards.

'I don't think there will be much bloodshed,' said Toby, as if he'd read his thoughts. 'My people are not as strong as the well-nourished mutants. And there are only about eighty functioning troops. The mutants number one hundred and nine. Leave them be. Come on. We must hurry.'

Through the metallic corridors they followed Toby until they came to the double doors which Jack recognised as the ones leading to the Governors' quarters.

Toby turned to look at him. 'Now,' he said, pushing open the great doors.

Inside, the Governing Seven looked up, startled.

Back in The Pit, the rest of the colony kept themselves busy. Elizabeth and Ashling worked themselves to exhaustion in an effort to keep their minds off the consequences if the assault failed. Now and then one of them would look up to see if a fleet of Cobians might be crossing the waste land to claim the rest of the earth people and the mutants.

'We have to be prepared for that, you know,' said Elizabeth. 'We have to accept the fact that they might lose. We may have to fight them off ourselves if they come here.'

'I know that,' said Ashling, looking around to make sure that Cara was out of earshot. 'I don't think I could go back there, Elizabeth. I couldn't face all that again.'

Elizabeth nodded. 'Me neither,' she said.

'I'd fight,' went on Ashling. 'I'd fight to ... to the death.'

'Don't think like that,' said Elizabeth. 'We musn't lose hope.'

But each of them knew that hope was very slim.

Elizabeth had set up a make-shift clinic where she treated the minor ailments of the mutants, particularly the children who, she said, were amazingly similar to humans.

'It's almost as if this small fertile area is restoring the Cobians to what they once were,' she said. 'Look, some of those girls are almost as pretty as yourself, Ash.'

Ashling laughed. But she could see that a handful of younger mutants, the ones who had grown up in The Pit untouched by experiments and exposed to a certain amount of sun and fresh air, were indeed humanoid in appearance. They were also very bright and were easy to train. With Toby's help, Elizabeth now had a team of medics capable of tending to their own people. Zig and Zag numbered among those. By now they had mastered some words and had become an important part of the community.

Cara was sitting with her chin in her hands, idly drawing patterns with the toe of her shoe in the sand. Ashling sat down beside her.

'Well, kid,' she said.

She grunted something and went on drawing the patterns.

'Is this a private art show, or can anyone look?' asked Ashling.

Cara looked up at her. 'I wish I could have gone too,' she said.

Ashling went to put her arms around her, but she realised that would reduce the child's feeling of grown-up confidence. For all her tender years and her skinny little body, Cara had shown more pluck and fortitude than most people at home do in a lifetime. Cara was an OK kid.

'Me too,' Ashling said. 'But those who went are much

stronger than you or me, Cara. We'd probably be in the way.'

'I suppose. Do you think they'll come back?'

'Of course,' she hid her own doubts. 'Of course they will.' Behind her back, she crossed her fingers.

Later, at the sleep time, she fell exhausted into the bundle of cloth that was her bed, she tossed about in a fever of anxiety. For some reason she was far more frightened now than she had ever been in all the time she'd been on this planet. She looked at Cara and marvelled at her easy sleep.

It must have been hours later, after she'd slipped into an uneasy doze, that Ashling was startled by rushing footsteps. Elizabeth was shaking her gently.

'Ashling,' she said softly. 'There's something happening. The look-outs at the gate have sent back a warning. They've seen a distant cloud of dust.'

Within seconds Ashling was on her feet. 'Cara,' she called. 'Come on.'

Other mutants were making their way through the green jungle and across the waste land to the gateway. Nobody knew what to expect. Were the Cobians coming? Was it the others limping back in defeat? Nobody wanted to guess.

Elizabeth clutched Ashling and Cara to her as they waited. Then they heard it - the distant hum of engines.

'Oh no,' groaned Ashling. 'Engines! That means ...' her voice trailed off. Elizabeth hugged her closer. 'Remember what we said,' she whispered.

Ashling nodded. If any of them ran away now, it would cause a general panic which would gain nothing. She stood firm, clenching her fists. The cloud of dust got bigger and the first shuttles came into view. They were speeding in a line towards the platform. As they drew nearer, Ashling shut her eyes to spare herself the sight of emerging Cobians. With a shout, Cara broke away from her.

'Cara!' Ashling shouted. She gasped when she saw Dan and Lou get out of the first shuttle. Now another shuttle was opening and Dave got out. Ashling's wave of relief stopped short when she saw him followed by three of the Governors.

'Hi,' smiled Jack, getting out of the third shuttle. 'We're back and we've brought company.'

Eighteen

It seemed strange to be back in the complex, this time not as a frightened prisoner. Ashling had come with Elizabeth to help load up with medicines and instruments. Other teams were in other parts of the complex gathering necessary items. Elizabeth looked around the forbidding place.

'I'm glad that the sick Cobians have been moved away from this cheerless infirmary,' she said. 'The new atmosphere can only do them good.'

'Do you think they'll settle?' asked Ashling. 'The other Cobians. Do you think they'll settle, now that they've lost control?'

'Yes. I think they will, eventually,' replied Elizabeth. 'It will take them a while to conform to other ways and another lifestyle, but they're clever enough to see that that's where their survival is. Yes, they'll be all right.'

'Isn't it good that there were so few injuries in the battle?' said Ashling, struggling with a large box of vacuum packed capsules. 'It didn't last long enough for real bloodshed.'

'That's because Jack and Toby knew that if they got to the Governors and told them about developments in The Pit they'd have no choice but to concede.'

'Where are they now?' asked Ashling. 'The Governors?'

Elizabeth smiled. 'Well, they're hardly called Governors any more - they've been stripped of that honour. They have their own quarters and I suppose they will eventually be rehabilitated. But they'll never have power again. Nor will the other Cobians. The mutants outnumber them and are more powerful. Whoever was it told us that there were over a thousand Cobians left? More like five hundred - and most of those were ailing.'

'Well, Zig and Zag won't take any nonsense from them ... from the Cobians,' laughed Ashling. 'They seem to have appointed themselves as Generals in Chief of the prisoners.'

'Poetic justice,' Elizabeth said. 'How the mighty are fallen.'

They carried their packages down to the waiting shuttles which were being loaded with all kinds of useful items. Though the mutants still regarded the earth people with a certain wariness, there was a feeling of friendly security surrounding the whole colony. Cara had befriended several of the younger mutants and, watching them play a primitive form of volleyball, one almost forgot that their backgrounds were so totally different.

As they were driven back towards The Pit, Ashling cupped her chin in her hand and looked up into the outer sky through the bigger hole which Dan and his team had made with the laser beams. Out there, somewhere, was the farmyard with the rattling door. Out there were her parents, probably demented with worry. Or would they have given up all hope by now of ever seeing herself and Cara again? Dad, with his battered hat and green quilted jacket that smelled of hay and tobacco. Did he still go to poker on Wednesday nights? And Mam. Did she still dream of turning the old stable into a restaurant during the summer season? She was going to make a fortune and take them all to Euro-Disney, she used to say. Ashling bit her lip. Had life stood still out there since she and Cara and the others had been whipped away? She forced her eyes away. Something died inside her every time she looked into that hole in the dome. She became aware of Elizabeth watching her.

'Me too, Ashling,' she said simply. 'Me too.'

Ashling nodded. What was the point in tormenting

herself with thoughts of the home she once knew? This was her home now. These were her people. But, as she watched the mutant who was driving the shuttle she wished with all her heart that it was her dad's profile she was looking at from the back of the old Cortina.

The days had settled into a routine of work, eating and sleeping. The absence of threat and fear, along with the increased light and air, seemed to make everyone flourish. Teams of mutants, who had been engaged in research or engineering before their maiming experiments, commuted to the complex each day to resume the work they had been doing. Apparently these skilled ones - the last lot of experiments - had offered themselves for these experiments in a desperate attempt to try and save their own people. Their joy at seeing the possibilities for their planet gave them a whole new zeal.

Others were anxious to develop the new skills introduced by the earth people. Elizabeth was training a highly efficient medical team, Jack and Dan had a large group of eager farmers who were making further irrigation channels and planting the precious grain rescued from the complex. Lou and Ashling watched Dave draw pictures in the sand for a group of interested mutants. He was drawing domed houses which could be made from materials brought from the complex. These would replace the lean-to hovels.

'Who does he think he is?' muttered Lou. 'Sam bloody Stephenson?'

'Who's Sam Stephenson?' asked Ashling.

'An architect. Did those civic offices up near Christchurch.'

'Humpf,' muttered Ashling. 'Given the chance Dave would do a better ...'

Ashling broke off and looked angrily at Lou, then glanced back at Dave, head bent intently over his work. She suppressed her anger and smiled. She realised Lou wanted her to get angry so that he could bad-mouth Dave and reduce him in her eyes.

'That's exactly what Dave is,' she said. 'He's an architect.'

Her dignity seemed to annoy Lou.

'What does an ex-con know about ..?' he began.

Ashling got up. 'Drop dead, Lou,' she said. 'Go and flex a bicep somewhere.'

Lou watched her leave and punched the sand with his fist. After a while he wandered over to Dave. Dave looked up at him, as if expecting the usual put-down.

'Is there anything I can do to help?' asked Lou.

Ashling was watching a group of Cobians being taught the methods of digging furrows for planting seeds. Now that they could see the efforts being made to save their planet, the hostilities between themselves and the mutants were gradually diminishing and they seemed anxious to learn these new ways. Some of the mutants who worked in the complex had returned. Led by Toby, they hurried over to where Jack was measuring out seeds into individual bags. The talk was animated and caused Jack to drop the bag he was holding.

Ashling sighed. Not more trouble, she hoped. Not now.

Jack made his way quickly to the medical centre.

'Toby,' Ashling was almost afraid to ask. 'Is something wrong?'

Toby came towards her. 'I've just had a report from the engineers who've been working on the space craft,' he said. 'The ship that brought you here is ready for a return journey.'

Ashling's mouth fell open. 'What do you mean, Toby?' she asked hesitantly.

Toby's reptilian mouth stretched into a grin.

'You're going home,' he said.

Nineteen

Cara was dancing around with excitement. She seemed to be more thrilled about the journey in the space craft than in actually going home - especially since Toby had told her she could sit in the control chamber.

'Isn't that cool, Ash?' she said.

Ashling nodded and looked at Jack and Elizabeth. They were sitting together, holding hands.

'Are you sure you won't change your minds?' she asked.

Elizabeth shook her head and laughed. 'Can't you see what we're achieving here, Ashling?' she said. 'There's a whole world here to be saved.'

'Besides, what would we go back to?' asked Jack. 'Me to my farm - with all the worries of whether the EU is going to clamp more stupid rules about what I can or cannot grow and how much milk my cows are permitted to yield? My sister is as good a farmer as anyone. She'll look after the place. Maybe she'll marry again and have a family. I hope she does,' he looked at Elizabeth. 'Everyone deserves a loving companion.'

'Get away with you,' laughed Elizabeth. 'You sound like a prudish old Victorian.' She became serious again. 'I think we'll be happy here, Ashling,' she went on. 'Yes sure, I could go back to ... to Rwanda or some other war-torn or drought-ridden country, but this is a different sort of challenge and every bit as important. Now that conditions here are gradually returning to what they once were, my particular medical knowledge will be pretty vital. Can you understand that? Can you understand why I want to stay?'

'I suppose,' said Ashling. 'I'll miss you both. I really will.'

'And we'll miss you,' said Elizabeth. 'All of you. But,' she looked up at Jack again, 'we have one another.'

'And we'll be spoiled rotten by Zig and Zag,' added Jack. The two seal creatures liked to treat the earth group as their personal property and couldn't seem to do enough for them.

Dan was busy gathering up and labelling samples of soil to bring home. Already boxes of the green vegetables had been stored in the craft, along with scientific notes and photographs.

'There's enough stuff here to make our lot at home sit up and think,' said Dan.

'Just make sure they do that,' said Jack. 'Make absolutely sure they act on all this information.'

Ashling wandered outside to where Dave was sitting with Zig and Zag. He grinned when he saw her and pointed to the symbols he was drawing in the sand.

'I've been telling them about the trip home,' he said. Ashling looked at the drawing. 'See,' continued Dave, 'this circle with the two seal bods and the bug-eyed Cobian represents this place. This oblong thing is the space craft, and the arrow pointing to this other circle is the journey back to earth.'

'And those stick insects are us?' Ashling pointed to the drawing of the craft. Dave nodded. 'There are only four earth people drawn in the space craft,' observed Ashling. 'You've left out the fifth person. Here, let me draw in the fifth. You can't even count..' she was laughing.

Dave put his hand over hers to prevent her drawing.

'It's the right count,' he said. 'I'm not going, Ashling.'

'What? Dave. you can't mean that ..!'

'Look at me, Ashling,' he smiled. 'I'm a changed person. For the first time in my life I mean something. I'm needed, and it's a nice feeling. I haven't had a rotten vibe since I started work with my two outsize buddies here.' He playfully slapped Zag and was rewarded with a toothy grin. 'What's there for me back home? I'd be back in the nick learning to crack safes or else shuffling in a dole queue, being snapped at by some biddy. No thanks. I feel good here. I'm ... I'm alive and useful.'

Ashling was shaking her head. 'Please come back with us, Dave. You could go on a course, learn a skill. You could stay with us. My parents would welcome you. We'd love to have you. I'd love to have you with us,' she added shyly.

'Don't try to coax me, Ashling. It wouldn't work. Here, in this place, we're all thrown together as ... as equals. Back home there's a different set of rules. No,' he held up his hand as Ashling tried to protest. 'You know as well as I do that we belong to completely different backgrounds - and people wouldn't be long about pointing that out. The world wouldn't let us forget that I'm an ex-con, a trouble-maker, and you're a nice, middle-class girl. Things are different up here, but our old world stays the same.'

'I'll stay then,' said Ashling. 'I'll stay and the world won't have anything to do with us ...'

'Don't do this, Ashling,' Dave was twisting his earring like he always did when he was nervous. 'Go on back. Just remember me as I am now, not as the geek I was until recently. Tell them back home how Dave the Dregs turned into someone half decent.'

'You're not Dave the Dregs,' said Ashling. 'And you're much more than half decent. Always were, but never got a chance to show it. Please won't you come back?' But she knew he'd made up his mind. He brushed at a mud stain on his shoe.

'You put me right,' he said.

'Me?'

'Yes. That time you came over and sat beside me when the others were acting the fool. You made me see through my own black cloud. From then on I started to look outside myself. Look, I can talk. Before, at home, I only grunted at people. You were right - I seemed to think everyone was out to get me. Here I talk and people listen. It's not just the mutants who are changing, it's this alien too,' he laughed and pointed to himself. 'Can't you see how I'm becoming more human now that I'm away from earth? Ironic, isn't it?'

Ashling smiled sadly. 'I suppose,' she grudgingly agreed. 'I'll never forget you, Dave.'

'And I certainly never will forget you,' he said and pressed her hand.

'Hey, don't look so glum. It's not really good bye, you know.'

She looked up at him with a puzzled expression. 'It's only o ... o ... what do the French say?'

'Au revoir.'

'That's the one. Well, it's only au rev whats it. I intend to become an engineer on one of those space craft. Toby said he'd teach me. Some dark night in a few years, I'll land in your father's field. I really will, Ashling. Wait and see.'

'I will, Dave,' she said earnestly. 'I'll wait.'

'No kidding,' he was equally earnest. 'I'll come for you when we have made this world green and sunny again. We're not saying goodbye. Just know that.'

'Ashling!' Cara ran over excitedly. 'Come on and see the space craft. You too, Dave. Come on! Jeepers, I can't wait to tell my class about it.'

Ashling marvelled at her young sister's ability to begin thinking of earthly things already.

There was a crowd gathering around the space craft. It looked enormous and Ashling felt a strange confusion of emotions as she contemplated getting on board. On the one hand she felt a deep bond of love for these people, Dave, Jack, Elizabeth and even the mutants, who had been her family for, how long now? Especially Dave. She looked over at him and her heart lurched. On the other hand she wanted to be home again in the Aga-warm kitchen, to look up and see her parents sitting in the comfortably shabby easy chairs watching the news on telly. Security. Would she ever feel secure again? Certainly life would never be the same.

Jack had his hand on Elizabeth's shoulder.

'Send us a postcard,' he said.

'I'll beam it up,' said Ashling.

'And ... grow up well,' he added.

'Ashling has already grown up,' Elizabeth smiled, giving Ashling a knowing, affectionate look.

'And Cara,' Jack called out as the eager child ran up the steps. 'Make them clean up the earth before they destroy it. Save the world, lass.'

'I will,' she shouted.

Lou paused to stand beside Ashling on the steps. 'Just think,' he said. 'All the publicity that's ahead of us when we get back.'

Ashling smiled. The old Lou was already reverting back to his image making. Maybe it was just as well that some things remained the same. She looked over to where Dave was standing with Zig and Zag.

'Watch out for twinkling stars,' he called. 'Because one night, in a few years, one of them will be me coming for you.' He grinned and gave her a thumbs-up sign. Ashling laughed through the tears she was fighting when the two seal creatures did the same. With one last look at them all, she turned to enter the space craft.

The End

THE BRIGHT SPARKS FAN CLUB

WOULD YOU LIKE TO JOIN?

Would you like to receive a **FREE** bookmark and BRIGHT SPARKS friendship bracelet?

You are already halfway there. If you fill in the questionnaire on the opposite page and one other questionnaire from the back page of any of the other BRIGHT SPARKS titles and return both questionnaires to Attic Press at the address below, you automatically become a member of the BRIGHT SPARKS FAN CLUB.

If you are, like many others, a lover of the BRIGHT SPARKS fiction series and become a member of the BRIGHT SPARKS FAN CLUB, you will receive special discount offers on all new BRIGHT SPARKS books, plus a BRIGHT SPARKS bookmark and a beautiful friendship bracelet made with the BRIGHT SPARKS colours. Traditionally friendship bracelets are worn by friends until they fall off! If your friends would like to join the club, tell them to buy the books and become a member of this book lovers' club.

Please keep on reading and spread the word about our wonderful books. We look forward to hearing from you soon.

Name ______________________________

Address ____________________________

____

Age _______________________________

Attic Press hopes you enjoyed *Saving the Dark Planet.* To help us improve the **Bright Sparks** series for you please answer the following questions.

1. Why did you decide to buy this book?

___

2. Did you enjoy this book? Why?

___

3. Where did you buy it?

___

4. What do you think of the cover?

___

5. Have you ever read any other books in the **BRIGHT SPARKS** series? Which one/s?

___

6. Have you any comments to make on the books in the **BRIGHT SPARKS** series?

___

If there is not enough space for your answers on this coupon please continue on a sheet of paper and attach it to the coupon.

Post this coupon to **Attic Press**, 29 Upper Mount Street, Dublin 2 and we'll send you a **BRIGHT SPARKS** bookmark.

Name____________________________Age_____
Address____________________________
____________________________Date________